"We can't afford to let our guard down till Evigan's back behind bars."

"No, we definitely can't." A look of apprehension flashed across Nikki's face. "So, what now?"

"I stick around for as long as it takes while the man remains a fugitive." Gavin jutted out his chin. "If that's all right with you...?"

Nikki nodded thoughtfully. "It has to be," she said in no uncertain terms. "I just want this over so I can get on with my life without needing to look over my shoulder."

Or having to deal with me and our shared and tragic history, Gavin mused. "I understand." He resisted the urge to touch Nikki's face, imagining how soft it would feel to his fingertips.

MISSISSIPPI MANHUNT

R. BARRI FLOWERS

In memory of my cherished mother, Marjah Aljean, a devoted lifelong fan of Harlequin romance novels, who inspired me to excel in my personal and professional lives. To H. Loraine, the true love of my life and best friend, whose support has been unwavering through the many terrific years together; and Carole Ann Jones, who left an impact on me with her incredible talents on the screen; as well as the loyal fans of my romance, mystery, suspense and thriller fiction published over the years. Lastly, a nod goes out to my amazing editors, Allison Lyons and Denise Zaza, for the wonderful opportunity to lend my literary voice and creative spirit to the Harlequin Intrigue line.

PLEASE RECYCLE • THIS PRODUCT IS RECYCLABLE •

Recycling programs for this product may not exist in your area.

ISBN-13: 978-1-335-45689-2

Mississippi Manhunt

For questions and comments about the quality of this book, please contact us at CustomerService@Harlequin.com.

Harlequin Enterprises ULC
22 Adelaide St. West, 41st Floor
Toronto, Ontario M5H 4E3, Canada
www.Harlequin.com

Printed in Lithuania

R. Barri Flowers is an award-winning author of crime, thriller, mystery and romance fiction featuring three-dimensional protagonists, riveting plots, unexpected twists and turns, and heart-pounding climaxes. With an expertise in true crime, serial killers and characterizing dangerous offenders, he is perfectly suited for the Harlequin Intrigue line. Chemistry and conflict between the hero and heroine, attention to detail and incorporating the very latest advances in criminal investigations are the cornerstones of his romantic suspense fiction. Discover more on popular social networks and Wikipedia.

Books by R. Barri Flowers

Harlequin Intrigue

The Lynleys of Law Enforcement

Special Agent Witness
Christmas Lights Killer
Murder in the Blue Ridge Mountains
Cold Murder in Kolton Lake
Campus Killer
Mississippi Manhunt

Hawaii CI

The Big Island Killer
Captured on Kauai
Honolulu Cold Homicide
Danger on Maui

Chasing the Violet Killer

Visit the Author Profile page at Harlequin.com.

CAST OF CHARACTERS

Nikki Sullivan—A successful artist, living in Owl's Bay, Mississippi, who survived after being kidnapped ten years ago by serial killer Perry Evigan, who murdered her best friend, Brigette Fontana. Could the prison escapee come after Nikki again?

Gavin Lynley—A special agent for the Mississippi Department of Corrections, he is tasked with protecting Nikki while her former abductor remains at large. The assignment is made more difficult by the fact that Gavin blames Nikki for the murder of his then-girlfriend, Brigette, at the hands of Evigan. Can they bury their differences for a new beginning?

Brooke Reidel—A detective for the Owl's Bay Police Department, committed to solving a string of local murders that appear to be linked to the dangerous inmate on the loose.

Marvin Whitfield—Director of investigations at MDOC, he is resolute in recapturing the escaped convicts, with his own credibility and ambitions on the line.

Jean O'Reilly—An MDOC special agent who is as dedicated to locating the fugitive Evigan as he is to keeping Nikki out of harm's way.

Perry Evigan—An escaped serial killer, dubbed the Gulfport Nightmare Killer, he is determined to claim the life of the one who got away, whatever it takes.

Prologue

Nikki Sullivan was admittedly bored to death on this summertime Saturday night as she paced lazily around her cozy, minimally furnished third-story apartment in Gulfport, Mississippi. An artist, one year removed from receiving a Bachelor of Arts degree from the University of Mississippi, she wasn't especially in the mood to do any canvases. She was single again after kicking her cheating and financially strapped boyfriend, Felix Kovell, to the curb two weeks earlier and was the better for it. She debated whether or not to call her best friend, Brigette Fontana, to see if she wanted to hang out or something. Brigette was currently in a relationship with Gavin Lynley, whom Nikki found to be incredibly good-looking and otherwise drenched in masculinity, while ever attentive to his girlfriend. But one would never know these admirable qualities in the man, based on Brigette—who was stunning herself—seemingly taking him for granted while having a roving eye on other guys, believing there was more than enough of her to go around. And around again whenever Gavin wasn't looking. Or was otherwise preoccupied. Though Nikki felt bad for him, she thought it wasn't her place to come between them and expose

Brigette. Much less suggest to him that he could do better than her in a partner. Even if he could.

He'll find out sooner or later and then can decide for himself, Nikki told herself, fantasizing that maybe they could even wind up together someday—assuming things didn't work out between him and Brigette. Before she could call her friend, having lifted the cell phone from the back pocket of her midrise skinny jeans, Nikki received a call from Brigette instead.

"I was just thinking about you," Nikki confessed truthfully, feeling a tad guilty as well in thinking about Gavin in romantic terms.

"Hopefully, good thoughts," Brigette joked, none the wiser.

"Of course," Nikki claimed, sitting on her leather sofa, folding her legs beneath her.

"So, what are you up to?"

"Not much. You?"

"I was supposed to go out with Gavin, but something came up and he canceled." She muttered an expletive in displeasure.

"Sorry to hear that," Nikki said, and truly meant it. But she knew that Gavin worked in corrections and sometimes, maybe more often than not, duty called. Even when he might have wished otherwise.

"Doesn't mean I need to sit here and mope about it," Brigette grumbled. "Let's go out and have some fun."

"What did you have in mind?" Nikki switched the phone to her other ear deliberately. "We could hang out here and watch some TV," she suggested. Or not.

"I'd rather do a few shots and some dancing," her friend countered. "Are you game?"

Nikki considered it for a moment or two before realizing how persuasive Brigette could be. Not to mention feeling antsy herself in wanting to get out of the stuffy apartment. Both were twenty-three, with Nikki having reached that age exactly two weeks ago. "Count me in," she agreed.

"Cool. I can be at your place in ten minutes or less."

"I'll be ready," Nikki promised and disconnected. She stood and shut her blue eyes for a moment as Nikki pulled her long light blond hair out of the low ponytail it was in, before changing into what she believed to be more suitable clothes for going out.

When Brigette arrived in her white Audi A3—recently purchased after the Arkansas State University graduate landed a job as an event coordinator with a prestigious public relations agency—Nikki hopped in. Taking one look at her gorgeous friend, who had bold apple-green eyes, mounds of wavy raven hair and a stunning body to kill for, Nikki found herself somewhat envious and sad at the same time that Brigette never seemed to appreciate what she brought to the table as a person, and could lose if she wasn't careful.

"So, where are we going?" Nikki asked coolly.

"I know the perfect place," Brigette answered evasively, and took off.

Nikki chuckled, ill at ease. "You're scaring me." She wasn't sure if it was from the speed at which her friend was driving, the mystery of where they were headed, or both.

"Really?" Brigette laughed and seemed to go even faster down the narrow street. "Where's your sense of adventure, girl?"

"Guess I'm about to find out," she relented, sucking in a calming breath.

They drove to a nightclub on Pickford Street called Johnnie's Shack in a seedy part of town, again giving Nikki some fresh concern. "You sure about this?"

"It'll be fine," Brigette promised. "Relax. I've been here a couple of times. We won't stay long."

"Okay." Nikki followed her friend's lead this time and went inside, where they did some tequila shots and then stepped onto a small dance floor and danced together to an upbeat song, before a tall, muscular man joined them and danced with them. He was in his early thirties and not too hard on the eyes, with defined features, dark eyes, medium-length brown hair in a windblown pompadour and an aquiline nose. He wore a multicolored plaid shirt and black distressed jeans.

He flashed a crooked smile and said affably, "I'm Perry."

Brigette smiled back flirtatiously. "I'm Brigette and this is my friend Nikki."

"Nice to meet you ladies." He grinned again and continued to move his Chukka boots to the music. "Hope you don't mind if I dance with you?"

Though Nikki's radar suddenly went up that he was being a bit too friendly and getting in their space—or putting it simply, he was bad news—Brigette apparently felt just the opposite, seemingly forgetting all about the fact that she had a boyfriend in Gavin, and told Perry enthusiastically, "Why not?"

After leaving the dance floor ten minutes later, he joined them at their table for more drinks, but didn't try to put the moves on either of them. Nikki still felt that something was off with the man, even if she couldn't quite put a finger on it in so many words, and convinced a reluctant Brigette that it was time to go. With no invitation for Perry to join them. When he thankfully put up no argument, remaining at the table as they left, Nikki thought they were home free of the potential threat. It was only when she began to feel light-headed in the dimly lit parking lot, and noticed the same with Brigette, that it became painfully obvious they had been drugged.

By who? Perry?

Nikki had her answer, as she watched the man in question picking Brigette up off the ground, where she had collapsed, and tossing her like a sack of potatoes in the back of a black Ford E-250 Super Duty cargo van. Then he did the same to her as, barely able to stand on wobbly legs, Nikki was unable to resist him before she passed out in his muscular arms. The last thing to enter her mind was whether or not she or Brigette would survive the night and the monster who had taken them against their will in a manner reminiscent of the serial killer who had been on the prowl in town.

PERRY EVIGAN COULDN'T help but chuckle with delight as he drove his latest captives back to the house he lived in on Robinson Road. Sitting on two acres of grassy land, it was far enough away from neighbors to allow him to come and go freely without attracting too much attention. He'd been planning on drugging and bringing back a single person for his trouble. He hadn't counted on two women for the price of one for him to have his way with before killing them and disposing of them as he had his other victims.

But there they were, ripe for the taking like apples off the tree—for which he was only too happy to oblige.

Admittedly, he could tell that the one calling herself Nikki was suspicious of him from the start. For a minute there, he thought with her watching him like a hawk, he'd never get the chance to spike their drinks with gamma-hydroxybutyrate. Thankfully, her attractive friend Brigette was more amenable to them hanging out together—even to the point of allowing him to buy the next round of drinks and pick them up—which, unfortunately, would prove to be a big error in judgment, as both women would soon regret having ever laid their pretty eyes on him once he was done with them. Something told him they were already regretting this, as he glanced at the two still-unconscious women lying in the back of the van. It had been almost too easy to slip the GHB into the drinks and then watch coolly as they sipped innocently on them while laughing at his stale jokes to keep them occupied. All he needed to do was let the two leave of their own accord for all to see and then pretend to leave casually on his own afterward and abduct them as they passed out, with no one being the wiser. He would come back later for the vehicle they drove in to the bar.

Arriving at the two-story, two-bedroom Greek Revival-style house with a shed and woods out back, he carried the women, one by one, inside the residence, where he lived alone but always welcomed the right company. Soon, the fun would begin. At least for him. For them, he had to admit with a laugh within, not so much.

THE NIGHTTIME RAID by heavily armed FBI agents and Gulfport Police Department detectives and SWAT Team, supported by Harrison County Sheriff's Office investigators from the Criminal Investigation Division and K-9 Patrol dogs, on the house on Robinson Road, led to the arrest of suspected serial killer Perry Evigan. The nude body of a woman identified as twenty-three-year-old Brigette Fontana was discovered in a bedroom. She had been sexually assaulted and strangled to death, barehanded, by Evigan, according to the autopsy report two days later.

Another woman, Nikki Sullivan, who had been abducted by Evigan at the same time outside Johnnie's Shack nightclub, and was described as a good friend of Ms. Fontana's, survived the vicious attack. Upon her full recovery, Ms. Sullivan was expected to testify against her attacker, dubbed the "Gulfport Nightmare Killer," who was believed to have strangled to death at least ten women over an eight-month span within the city of Gulfport, Mississippi, Harrison County's co-county seat.

Chapter One

During a violent nighttime uprising at the Mississippi State Penitentiary in Sunflower County, Mississippi, three hard-core inmates seized on the opportune distraction to stage a dramatic getaway. After quickly overwhelming prison guards, the trio made a daring escape from Area I of the maximum-security prison on Parchman Road known as Parchman Farm.

The leader of the escapees, a convicted murderer, spotted a red GMC Sierra 1500 parked not far from the prison. Its driver, a lanky, thirtysomething, baldheaded male, was talking on a cell phone, seemingly oblivious to his surroundings. Or the potential peril present. Once the inmates had his attention, it was too late for him to deny them what they wanted: his vehicle and the phone. Unfortunately, leaving behind a witness to their car theft wasn't in the cards. Strangling the man to death with his own leather belt was easy for the ringleader. After all, he'd had lots of experience using this method to kill others. And if things went as planned, he fully intended to pick up where he left off years ago.

Starting with the pretty one who escaped death before he could squeeze the life out of her.

The prisoners climbed into the pickup truck and headed

west on Highway 32 toward the city of Ruleville, Mississippi. There, they would get a change of clothing, food, money and maybe switch cars, before fleeing the area entirely, ahead of the correctional authorities and other law enforcement personnel's determined efforts to recapture them. Or do whatever it took to prevent the dangerous fugitives from living in the free world again.

SPECIAL AGENT GAVIN LYNLEY of the Mississippi Department of Corrections, Corrections Investigation Division's Special Operations Unit, removed the FN 509 MRD-LE 9mm semiautomatic pistol from the tactical thigh holster as he cautiously approached the black Hyundai Sonata. It was parked outside a ranch-style home on Frinton Street in Vicksburg, Mississippi. A run on the license plate confirmed that the vehicle belonged to Titus Malfoy, a probation officer for the MDOC, who was wanted for embezzling money from probationers. The victims were working to pay off their debts to the court as required in the terms for regaining freedom. Instead, an internal investigation revealed that Malfoy pocketed what wasn't his to have at their expense, resulting in longer sentences for those victimized unsuspectingly.

Gavin glanced at the other side of the vehicle, where Special Agent Jean O'Reilly, her gun drawn, was also prepared to act should the suspect behind the steering wheel make the wrong move. Peering at the probation officer, who was talking on his cell phone, recognizing him, Gavin said with an edge to his voice, "Step out of the car and keep your hands where I can see them."

Looking surprised, Titus Malfoy cut the call short and complied with the order. He opened the door carefully and climbed out. "What's this all about?" he demanded as his brow creased in three irregular lines as though totally perplexed.

Gavin noted that they were about the same height of six feet and three inches. But he was in better shape than Malfoy, who was African American, a year younger at thirty-five than the man, had darker and shorter hair than the probation officer, who had a bleached high top and textured dreads, and was gray-eyed compared to the brown color of the suspect's eyes, which were shifting nervously. "Titus Malfoy, you're under arrest for embezzlement and abusing your position as a probation officer."

"What?" Malfoy cocked a thick brow of denial. "This has to be some kind of mistake."

"I don't think so." Gavin was confident that the months-long investigation of his crimes was spot-on. He frisked the man and found that he didn't have a firearm or other weapon on him. "You messed up big time, Malfoy," he told him bluntly. "Now you'll have to answer for it."

Agent O'Reilly, slender and thirtysomething with long crimson hair in a tight bun, big blue eyes and fresh off a divorce, handcuffed the suspect behind his back and said skeptically, "If you're really innocent, you'll have ample opportunity to prove it. If not, you could be looking at decades behind bars. Sorry." Her tone indicated the apology was sarcastic rather than sincere.

As Malfoy muttered an expletive in response, Gavin told him tersely, "Let's go." He wondered just how many more bad apples they would discover in the probe of corruption within the ranks of the Mississippi Department of Corrections. It was troubling, to say the least, as he wanted to believe that this was just an isolated problem and not broad in scope for an organization that Gavin had been employed with for more than a decade. Or ever since shortly after he had received his undergraduate degree in Criminology from Mississippi State University, and followed the long tradition of family members who made careers for themselves in law enforcement.

Gavin led the suspect to the official CID vehicle they had driven to the scene, a dark ash metallic Chevrolet Tahoe SUV. Malfoy was put in the back seat, then Gavin sat in the front passenger seat, while Jean got behind the wheel and drove to the Vicksburg Police Department on Veto Street, where the suspect was turned over for processing.

Afterward, they took a mostly silent forty-five-mile drive to the Mississippi Department of Corrections Central Office headquarters on North Lamar Street in Jackson, where the report was filed on the arrest of Titus Malfoy, and Gavin settled into his office for some follow-up work. He was at a height-adjustable standing desk, glancing at his laptop, when the Director of Investigations at MDOC, Marvin Whitfield, strode in. He had an iPad in his hands.

Whitfield, African American, was in his forties, medium height and solidly built, with a short and tapered black Afro and sable eyes. “Good job, Lynley, with Agent O’Reilly, in taking Malfoy into custody without incident,” he said, squaring his shoulders inside the jacket of his crisp navy suit worn with black plain leather Derbys.

“I wish it hadn’t come down to that,” Gavin said, twisting his lips in despair. He knew that the arrest indicated that one of their own had crossed the line, implicating the entire department to one degree or another by association. If not guilt.

"Yeah, I know what you mean." Whitfield pinched his broad nose. "But it is what it is… Unfortunately, we've got other problems to deal with." He paused, ill at ease. "Last night there was a riot at the Mississippi State Penitentiary."

"Yeah, I heard about it." Gavin recalled the news about an uprising at the prison related to conditions that had been described by some as deplorable. From what limited information he gathered, at least one inmate had been killed and several injured, before guards were able to bring things under control.

"While conducting an emergency head count at five this morning, it was discovered that three inmates were missing." Whitfield sighed noisily. "They took advantage of the melee and killed one guard—Stan MacGregor, age thirty-nine, who was married with four kids—while seriously wounding another, before the trio managed to flee the prison grounds. Along the way, the escapees stole a pickup truck after killing the driver, thirty-four-year-old Jason Ollero."

"Wow." Gavin felt terrible for the guards attacked, as well as the pickup driver, who was obviously in the worst place at the worst time. He hoped the injured guard pulled through.

"It gets worse," the longtime director muttered. "One of the escaped inmates is Perry Evigan…"

"What?" Gavin's heart sank into his stomach, even as Whitfield reiterated this disturbing news, and showed him Evigan's mug shot on the tablet. Seeing his chiseled face and foreboding hazel eyes, along with closely cropped brown-gray hair, gave Gavin the creeps.

"Yeah, freaks me out too," Whitfield muttered. He identified the other escapees as Craig Schneider and Aaron Machado, pulling their images up on the tablet.

Gavin glanced at Schneider, who was white, round-faced and blue-eyed, with a black crew cut and anchor beard. Machado was Latino, baldheaded, smooth-shaven, triangular-faced and had dark brown eyes. While noting their appearances, Gavin's focus was squarely on Perry Evigan. Ten years ago, Evigan raped and murdered Gavin's then-girlfriend, Brigette Fontana. She was strangled to death by him. Known as the Gulfport Nightmare Killer, Evigan had killed a total of ten young women by ligature strangulation in and around Gulfport. Brigette was his last homicide victim, who was abducted by the killer along with Brigette's best friend, Nikki Sullivan. Though she survived the kidnapping and attempted rape, Nikki was left with a broken jaw, busted lower lip, seriously sprained ankle and a concussion—along with the psychological wounds she sustained during her victimization—before being rescued by the authorities from Evigan's house.

Perry Evigan himself—a then-thirty-four-year-old divorcé and journeyman, with a dark fixation on such serial killers as the so-called Boston Strangler, believed by many to be serial rapist Albert DeSalvo, and cousins Kenneth Bianchi and Angelo Buono Jr., known as the Hillside Stranglers—was taken into custody, in spite of Evigan's resisting arrest. He would eventually be convicted for his crimes and sentenced to spend the rest of his life in prison. Until now.

"Do we know where they are?" Gavin asked the director tartly, hating the thought that Evigan was tasting freedom for even a second, after what he'd done.

"Unfortunately, not at the moment." Whitfield furrowed his forehead. "They made their way to Ruleville and ditched the pickup. We're not sure what they're driving now. We have the department's Fugitive Apprehension Strike Team and K-9 unit trying to track them down, with assistance from the FBI and US Marshals Service, along with the Jackson Police Department, Sunflower County Sheriff's Office and surrounding law enforcement agencies on full alert. We'll get them back," he said confidently. "But until such time, we need to protect the one woman who miraculously managed to survive Perry Evigan's attempt to sexually assault and murder her from being added to his list of fatalities. That's where you come in, Lynley—"

Putting aside his conflicting thoughts at the moment, Gavin met the director's eyes sharply. "You want me to be a bodyguard?" Even when questioning him, Gavin knew it was not nearly that simple.

"I want you to keep the person alive whose critical testimony helped put Evigan away, ensuring that he would spend the rest of his miserable life behind bars." Whitfield drew a breath. "At least that was our intention. Now he's out there somewhere, free as a bird, and just might try to track down Nikki Sullivan, insane as that sounds. But we can't put anything past Evigan, who, as I recall, singled out Ms. Sullivan as his one regret—not killing her when he had the chance."

"I remember," Gavin muttered painfully, knowing it was hard to forget, all things considered.

"Maybe he wants a redo." Whitfield jutted his chin. "We can't let that happen. As a member of the Special Operations Unit, Lynley, we need to be able to occasionally provide protection, when warranted. This seems to be one of those times, with the prisoners' escape under our jurisdiction. As you and Ms. Sullivan share a common bond with Evigan's last murder victim, Brigette Fontana, this assignment should be right up your alley. Am I right?"

Gavin hesitated in his response. Normally, he would have agreed with this assessment. How could he not, given the situation as it were? But in this instance, he had an undeniable large chip on his shoulder where it concerned Nikki Sullivan. He blamed her for placating Brigette's reckless desire to go out that night, leading her right into the crosshairs of Perry Evigan. Though Gavin admittedly blamed himself just as much, considering he had to work the night in question, preventing him from being with Brigette and presumably saving her life—he was certainly glad that Nikki had come out on the other side and been given the opportunity to move on with her life. This notwithstanding, being around her right now would only remind him of what he lost in Brigette and any future they might have had. And everything that could have come with that package—like a family and home together. Wasn't that where they were headed? But that wasn't exactly an acceptable excuse for not being able to do his job effectively. Was it? Even if that job meant reuniting with Brigette's best friend, in order to keep her safe from the same serial killer who put Brigette in the grave at the young age of twenty-three.

Gavin nodded at the director, maintaining his cool in the process. "Of course, I'll do my best to keep Ms. Sullivan out of harm's way while Evigan is still at large." *Hopefully, that will be of short duration, or Evigan could be apprehended even before I have to come face-to-face with Nikki for the first time in years*, Gavin told himself, knowing that the sooner they located the three escapees, the sooner they could wipe the proverbial egg off their faces in having to account for the escape in the first place on their watch.

"Good." Whitfield flashed him a satisfied look. "Of course, we'll need to locate Nikki Sullivan first—assuming she hasn't remained in the same place—wherever she might be if she's still in Mississippi after a decade, before Evigan can, and warn her about the possible danger to her life."

"I understand." Gavin had not kept track of Nikki's whereabouts after Evigan's trial and conviction. There had been no need to with neither on particularly good terms with the blame game. Both had gone their separate ways. But he had heard through the grapevine that Brigette's gorgeous, as he recalled, and talented artist friend had smartly moved from Gulfport and the dark memories left behind. Now he just had to find out where she was and make sure she remained safe till the escaped serial killer was back in custody where he belonged.

An hour later, after making a few phone calls and doing some double-checking, Gavin had his answer. Nikki Sullivan had relocated to Owl's Bay, a town in Yaeden County, about thirty miles down the coast from Gulfport and approximately one hundred and seventy miles from Jackson. Moreover, Owl's Bay was around three hundred miles from Ruleville, where Perry Evigan and the other escapees were last spotted. Though it seemed like a stretch that Evigan would try to make his way back to the area where he perpetrated his serial murders, if this were the case, he'd had a head start.

Gavin alerted authorities along US 49 South and I-55

South, leading into Owl's Bay from Ruleville, to be on the lookout, or BOLO, for the fugitives, who could be driving any type of vehicle while on the run. And that was under the assumption that they hadn't split up. For the moment, Gavin was more focused on Evigan, in particular, with his mug shot sent to the local law enforcement agencies. Should he be foolish enough to go after Nikki.

Against his better judgment, Gavin decided not to call Nikki, sure she'd hang up on his face. Freaking her out by leaving a disturbing message probably wasn't a good idea either. He assumed that she had heard about Evigan's escape and was taking precautions accordingly. *I don't want to spook her by leaving a text that her life could be in danger*, Gavin told himself, trusting that he could get to her in time to protect her. In the meantime, he would give the locals a heads-up on the situation as it related to Nikki Sullivan.

Gavin left the MDOC Central Office headquarters and climbed back into the Chevrolet Tahoe he had arrived in, then swung by his Louisiana-style house on a cul-de-sac on Heritage Hill Drive. He lived alone in the spacious two-story home that sat on two acres of land with mature landscaping and tall oak trees, but would gladly share it with the right person, were she to come into his life. He once thought that might be Brigette, but they were never allowed to put it to the test, before her life ended.

Stepping through the front door, Gavin headed across the vinyl plank flooring and up the straight staircase. He grabbed a few extra clothing items and toiletries, in case this assignment turned out to be longer than a day or two—stuffing them into a black leather tote bag—then headed back downstairs and out the door.

With any luck, Perry Evigan and the other escapees would be back in custody and a prison cell before Gavin ever arrived in Owl's Bay. He only wished he could take luck to the bank, where it concerned a ruthless serial killer on the loose and a woman from Gavin's past who potentially had a target on her back.

NIKKI SULLIVAN SAT in a club chair in the circle of a support group for survivors of traumatic events in the large backyard of the vintage home in the small Mississippi coastal town of Owl's Bay. She had participated off and on ever since relocating there from Gulfport eight years ago. She considered it a security blanket of sorts to be around others who had been left with permanent scars on their psyche—and in some cases, the accompanying physical scars—as a result of experiences they could never forget. Even if they tried. This was certainly true for her, even as she tried to distance herself by moving away from the scene of the crime and the man who unfairly blamed her for it.

Nikki trained her ocean-blue eyes on Blair Roxburgh, a trained psychologist and the homeowner who started the group, which currently consisted of six women and two men. She and Blair were both the same age of thirty-three and similarly slender in build, but Blair was a couple of inches shorter than Nikki's five-foot-seven-and-a-half height, and had a darker shade of blond in her short shag than Nikki's long and layered yellow locks that were fashioned in a blunt U-shaped cut. She listened as Blair retold her terrifying tale for the benefit of those new to the group.

"I was sexually assaulted as an eighteen-year-old college freshman," she said, her hazel eyes dampening as though thrust back in time to the moment the attack occurred. "My attacker was someone I thought I knew. Till he turned out to be someone entirely different—a monster hidden behind a handsome face. For the longest time, I blamed myself as many victims do when missing the warning signs that place you in danger, before gaining the courage to affix blame where it was due—squarely on the rapist himself." Blair took a moment to regain her composure. "We're all here today because of what we've been put through and are now survivors with a greater sense of self-worth and solace in knowing that we're not alone." She gazed warmly at Nikki and said even-toned, "Tell us your story, if you feel comfortable doing so."

Nikki smiled softly at her, having established a rapport that helped her feel at ease. "I'm Nikki Sullivan," she told the group in a well-practiced and affable tone. "Ten years ago, I was the victim of a brutal attack by a serial killer named Perry Evigan. He sexually assaulted and then strangled to death ten women, including my best friend, Brigette, after he drugged us. I was supposed to die too, but the FBI and local authorities miraculously came to my rescue before he could finish the job. I got lucky—if you could call it that—ending up with a broken jaw in two places, that still aches on occasion, a concussion, badly sprained ankle and a bloodied lower lip." She winced at the thought. "In spite of my best efforts to the contrary, the regrets about what happened and what I might have done differently if I could go back in time have never gone away. Or the nightmares." She sucked in a deep breath as Nikki mused about Perry Evigan, hating that he still had a hold on her somewhat as a sexual predator, even after all these years, and knowing he was safely put away in prison for the rest of his life. "Anyway, that's my story," she said, lifting her chin defiantly, "and, like everyone here, I'm a survivor and proud of it."

With that, there was applause and Nikki smiled, while knowing that the strength in numbers was what kept each of them going when left to themselves. And that the ebb and flow between sadness and empowerment would continue as each person recounted his or her experience. The last to speak was one of the male survivors, Harry Rosen, a forty-three-year-old US Air Force veteran, traumatized from his experiences when serving in Afghanistan. It cost him one of his legs. He finished by saying courageously, "It's been tough some days, for sure. But right here, right now, I can tell you that I'd enlist all over again in representing my country in the military."

More applause came before it swung back to Blair. After the group meeting was over and they were alone in the backyard, Nikki was approached by the counseling psychologist, who had become a trusted friend. Blair said to her, "Are you free for lunch?"

Nikki shook her head. "I can't," she responded reluctantly. "My latest artwork won't paint itself, if I'm going to have it ready for the showing on Saturday."

"Understood," Blair said. "Not a problem."

"Rain check?"

"You've got it."

Nikki smiled gratefully. "See you at the next meeting."

Blair patted her hand. "Wouldn't miss it," she joked.

Nikki laughed. "Didn't imagine you would."

"If I ever did, you could always fill in for me."

"You think?"

"Absolutely." Blair nodded. "Everyone likes you and

feels comfortable with you, which encourages them to talk about their ordeals."

"Hmm." Nikki flushed. "I'll keep that in mind."

She left the four-sided brick home on Aplen Avenue and headed for her car on this early afternoon with the sun shining brightly to remind her it was mid-July. She climbed inside the red Subaru Crosstrek and headed home, where she had her studio. Art had been her passion for as long as she could remember and Nikki had managed to turn it into a successful career over the years, specializing in landscape, still life and portrait oil paintings—with showings across the state and occasionally elsewhere.

She hadn't been nearly as successful with her love life. The few times she had dated someone over the years, Nikki had come up empty. That included a guy she had gone out on a date with exactly one time recently—a personal trainer named Kenan Fernández—only to find there was absolutely no chemistry whatsoever. He seemed to feel otherwise, but she had not seen him since, ignoring his phone and text messages.

The reality was that she had yet to find the right person to have a serious romance with. It left Nikki wondering if her standards were too high. Had her brush with death left her emotionally damaged? Or was it more about her unwillingness to take a chance on someone, only to fail and have her heart broken? Would that be more than she could take in only wanting a happy ending, after losing a friend to a serial killer?

Nikki's thoughts drifted away as her attention turned to the news brief on the radio. "According to the Mississippi Department of Corrections," the female broadcaster reported tensely, "in the midst of unrest at the Mississippi

State Penitentiary, three inmates managed a brazen escape in the wee hours of the morning, killing a guard and the driver of a pickup truck along the way. The escapees, all lifers for serious crimes of violence, have been identified as forty-four-year-old Perry Evigan, thirty-six-year-old Aaron Machado and Craig Schneider, age twenty-seven."

Nikki's heart skipped a beat at the mention of Perry Evigan's name, even as she heard the newscaster say in dramatic fashion, "Evigan, once dubbed the Gulfport Nightmare Killer, strangled to death ten women—sexually assaulting them beforehand—before being captured a decade ago. One woman was able to survive an attack by the serial killer and testified at his trial nearly nine years ago, resulting in a conviction and life sentence. The escapees are described as armed and extremely dangerous..."

What? Evigan is out of prison and on the loose, Nikki thought, the very notion shaking her to the core as her fingers trembled around the steering wheel. How could that have happened? He was supposed to be locked away forever in a maximum-security facility. With no escape possible. She shuddered in recalling Perry Evigan's haunting last words to her during his trial.

I'll see you again someday, Nikki, and finish what I started. Trust me.

She had totally rejected his threat as the ravings of a defeated and defiant man on his way back to prison. Was he now in a position to make good on that threat? she had to wonder. *Am I in danger*? Nikki asked herself, worried. Did she need to go into hiding while that bastard remained free? Or would the authorities, who, according to the news report, had intensified their search for the escaped convicts, have them back in custody long before Evigan could seriously entertain tracking her down nine years later?

Nikki mulled over this troubling development and the potentially high stakes for her own life, security and future, as she pulled into the driveway of her custom-built, three-bedroom Creole cottage-style home on Waconia Way, outside the garage. With a stunning backside view of the nearby Jourdan River, the property was bordered by sugar maple trees, giving her some privacy. Only when she got out of the car, did Nikki notice the dark-colored Chevrolet Tahoe parked across the street. Had it been there before? Did it belong to her neighbor?

A spasm of fear ripped through her, as the vehicle's driver-side door opened. Could Perry Evigan have already found her? Not that it would have been too difficult as she hadn't exactly tried to hide from him, per se, not believing she needed to. Picturing the smug face of the man who tried to kill her, Nikki's first instinct was to bolt for her front door, where she had a good security system inside that would protect her and alert the police. Short of that, she had a stun gun in her leather hobo bag to defend herself with. If that failed, she could always make use of the skills she'd learned in the self-defense courses she'd taken after her attack and refreshed herself with periodically.

When a tall and very fit male stepped out of the car, Nikki spied the somewhat familiar devilishly handsome face of a biracial man. One she never expected to see again, even if not necessarily her preference. Or maybe she had felt it was for the best, when considering the bad blood that had existed between them in the wake of Brigette's death. Now in his midthirties, he still had the taut oblong face, piercing gray eyes and slightly crooked mouth she had last seen right after Perry Evigan's trial ended. New was the five o'clock shadow beard and trendy style of his short raven hair in a midrazor fade. She stood there flat-footed as he quickly closed the distance between them in his boat shoes, to go with a light blue polo shirt and dark chinos. Her instinct to run away from him was stilled by curiosity, if nothing else.

"Nikki," he said tonelessly and paused. "It's been a minute."

"More like nine years," she said wryly to her late friend Brigette's former boyfriend, Gavin Lynley. Nikki fluttered her lashes. "What are you doing here?"

Gavin pinched his Roman nose and said without preface, "Perry Evigan has escaped from prison."

"I just heard it on the radio." Nikki's brow furrowed as she fought to maintain her composure. She was admittedly still piqued as to why Gavin needed—or even wanted, after the way they left things—to convey the news in person. Peering at him, she asked pointedly, "So, did you come to tell me that he's been recaptured?"

"I'm here to say I hope that will be a done deal shortly." Gavin glanced down at his shoes and then lifted his eyes to meet hers fixedly. "Until such time, I've been assigned to make sure Perry Evigan doesn't come anywhere near you."

Chapter Two

Gavin could tell that Nikki saw him as almost as much her enemy as Perry Evigan. Not that he could blame her any. The last time he had laid eyes upon her, they had parted as nothing but two people who had lost someone each cared about. They certainly hadn't moved in opposite directions on a positive note. Much less, as friends. Whether he cared to admit it or not, Gavin knew that he had to bear much of the blame for that. He had pushed Nikki away as the only person he knew with a direct line to Brigette when she was alive and, in theory, could have been a shoulder for Gavin to lean on. And vice versa.

But he had been too wounded at the time to think in those terms. All he wanted to do was try to put the past behind him—including Brigette's best friend, whom he'd been attracted to since the day they first met, but never acted on out of respect for Brigette in not wanting to cross any lines—and move on with his life. Clearly, this had been Nikki's intent too.

Till he unceremoniously reentered the picture. Thanks to their mutual foe: Perry Evigan.

Gavin studied her now, as Nikki glared at him with those enchanting royal blue eyes. They were beautiful, along with a delicate nose and generous mouth on a heart-shaped face, which had only gotten more attractive with time. The blunt cut of Nikki's long blond locks agreed with her. She was still appealingly slender and the perfect height in relation to his own, while wearing a peach-colored smocked-trim top, navy trouser pants and moccasin flats.

Now came the hard part. He needed to break the ice that had formed a thick barrier between them over the past nine years and at least try to remain cordial while keeping her out of harm's way.

"You're joking, right?" Nikki's eyes flashed hotly at him. "You've shown up out of nowhere to be my bodyguard? Maybe I'd be better off taking my chances with Perry Evigan. At least I know who I'm dealing with in him. As opposed to you, who outright accused me of being responsible for Brigette's death. My best friend. And never seemed to back down, as I recall. Now this?" Her lashes curled whimsically. "How did you expect me to react?"

Oh boy, this is going to be harder than I'd imagined, Gavin told himself, as he eyed her resting a hand on a slender hip. "Just the way you have," he had to confess. Or at the very least, he hadn't exactly expected a welcoming committee. He glanced about to assess the surroundings. Seemed pleasant enough, with mature cypress trees lining the streets and an otherwise peacefulness in the atmosphere. Unfortunately, this did little to make him feel at ease, fully aware that the facade would be perfect cover for a ruthless serial killer to go on the attack. Gavin turned back to Nikki and asked in a pleading tone, "Do you mind if we go inside and talk about this?" He looked over her head at the two-story cottage she called home.

Without uttering another word, Nikki turned and

headed up the walkway, inviting him with her silence to follow, which he did. On the front porch, there were two black wicker chairs that they bypassed.

Walking through the door, Gavin stepped onto the travertine floor and took in the Spanish Cedar millwork and open concept with a high ceiling, cottage-style ceiling fan and symmetrical windows with vinyl Venetian blinds. There was a good-size living and dining area, wicker furnishings, floating staircase and gourmet kitchen with a marble countertop and breakfast nook. He took note of the security system, as well as the double-cylinder deadbolt front door lock.

He gazed at Nikki and said sheepishly, "Nice place."

"Thanks," she responded tonelessly, her arms folded while waiting anxiously to hear more from him on the situation they found themselves in.

"Look, I know I'm probably the last person you expected to see show up at your house," Gavin conceded, "short of Perry Evigan. Truthfully, I wasn't expecting it either. But due to the circumstances..." He paused. "So, here's the deal..." Gavin knew there would be no sugarcoating this. So why try? "As a special agent with the Mississippi Department of Corrections, protecting crime victims and witnesses is part of my duties. Given that Perry Evigan was one of the escapees from our prison system and swore vengeance against you—and also happened to be responsible for the death of Brigette Fontana, my then-girlfriend—I suppose I was the obvious choice of my boss to keep you safe in the remote chance that Evigan manages to evade recapture and tries to make good on his threat."

"Obvious choice. Really?" Nikki pursed her lips skeptically. "Maybe not the best choice, given our strained history. To say the least."

Gavin found that hard to argue with on its merits. "I wanted to call to see if you were okay with this, but figured my best bet was to do it face-to-face," he said.

She reacted with a sneer. "I'm not so sure about that."

"Look, if having me around, even for a short while, really makes you uncomfortable, I can get the locals to assign an officer to protect you." Gavin met her eyes. "Until such time, I can wait outside till the officer arrives..."

Nikki seemed to weigh her options, before saying tentatively, "That won't be necessary. If this is your job, I suppose I can handle it, if you can."

He nodded in agreement. "I'm sure I'll be out of your hair in no time flat." Even in uttering the words, Gavin couldn't help but wonder what it would be like to run his fingers through that long luscious hair of hers.

"Fine." She took a breath. "Do you really think that Perry Evigan would risk his newfound freedom to try and find me after all these years?" she questioned.

It was something that Gavin had already asked himself more than once. Assuming Evigan still had a little common sense and even a little intelligence, it would seem improbable that he would roll the dice in coming for Nikki when he had to know that the risk would not likely justify the means. As it pertained to his staying on the lam successfully, it was a tough task under the best of circumstances. But something told Gavin that the psychopath in Evigan might well be driven by impulses beyond his own best interests. Or normal behavior.

Trying to keep it as diplomatic as possible, Gavin responded evenly, "Probably not. But the man is a serial killer and knows that with the high probability that he'll be caught sooner rather than later—he may feel he has nothing to lose and everything to gain, in trying to finish what he started ten years ago." Gavin reached out and touched her shoulder. He ignored the powerful sensation that this small gesture brought about, while telling her in earnest, "I won't let that happen."

Nikki gave a slow and grateful nod. "Thank you."

"Not a problem." Even if it had been, he wouldn't have admitted to this. He was on an assignment and owed it to her—and the shared memory of Brigette—to see it through, with minimal disruption of Nikki's life before walking away from her. Again. "So, are you still an artist?" The question was more conversational than anything. In the course of establishing her whereabouts and out of curiosity, Gavin had discovered that she had, in fact, made a name for herself in the local art world with prominent showings and paintings in high demand. Nikki had not used a pseudonym when relocating from Gulfport to Owl's Bay. Meaning that Evigan would likely have little trouble using social media or online news sources to discover her location, which concerned Gavin.

"Yes," she answered matter-of-factly. "Mostly landscape and still life, with some portraits."

"Nice." Gavin grinned, recalling how he had seen and admired some of her paintings back in the day when Brigette had insisted that he come along to check out a few that Nikki had laid out in her apartment. He imagined her work would be even more compelling today.

"Speaking of which—" Nikki broke into his thoughts "—I do need to get to my studio, down the hall, for some work. It will also keep my mind occupied on something other than Perry Evigan possibly trying to kill me… and—" she made an uncomfortable expression on her face "—sexually assaulting me beforehand, per his MO." She looked away. "Since you'll probably be here for a little while, I guess you can make yourself at home, Gavin. There are drinks and half an apple pie in the fridge, if you get thirsty or hungry. And the first-floor bathroom is just off the kitchen."

"Thanks." He appreciated the hospitality, even if Gavin didn't feel particularly welcomed and rightfully so. They'd had their differences and they wouldn't be resolved overnight. But that didn't mean they couldn't be nice to each other while occupying the same house. As soon as he got word that Evigan had been arrested and was no longer a threat to Nikki or anyone else, Gavin would get out of her life and they could each go about their business.

Or was this a good time to address the past and losing Brigette to senseless violence, once and for all?

He watched as Nikki walked away, before Gavin took out his cell phone and rang Marvin Whitfield. "I'm with her now," he told the director equably.

"No trouble?"

"Not yet," Gavin responded.

"Good. How's she doing with the news that Perry Evigan is out?" Whitfield asked.

"Probably as well as could be expected." Gavin glanced down the hall and saw that Nikki had gone into her studio. "Honestly, though she's put on a brave face, Nikki's spooked, and with good reason. Any word yet on the whereabouts of Evigan and the other escapees?"

"Reports have come in that the trio may have been spotted in Tennessee," Whitfield indicated. "But others claimed to have seen them in Alabama." The director sighed. "Right now, we don't have a solid fix on their whereabouts. With the head start the inmates had before we realized they were missing, Evigan, Machado and Schneider could be anywhere, frankly. They are believed to be driving a black Chrysler Pacifica that was stolen in Boyle. According to the elderly owner, Donald Takeuchi, who wasn't home at the time, the trio also broke into his house and stole two legally purchased firearms—a Glock G43X subcompact semiauto pistol and a SIG Sauer P365 9mm pistol, along with ammo."

"That's not very comforting," Gavin told him bluntly, though hardly surprised that the escapees would arm themselves while on the run. "Evigan and his killer pals are not likely to turn themselves in peacefully and miss out on their one big opportunity to escape to greener pastures. They could've left the state—which would have been the smartest move—or chosen to lay low in Mississippi, traveling the back roads while trying to bypass roadblocks they would have to get past in whatever stolen vehicle they were driving."

"Yeah, desperate as they are, there's no telling what their mindset is while trying to avoid capture," Whitfield voiced. "All we know for certain is that they're still on the loose, armed and extremely dangerous."

Gavin muttered words in agreement. "Which makes the situation all the more aggravating and frightening."

"Just keep Ms. Sullivan safe," the director ordered, "till we can bring in Evigan, in particular, as well as Machado and Schneider."

"Will do," Gavin promised. Even if Nikki would probably still prefer another person to be her protector. Or had she begun to let her guard down a bit with him—and vice versa—in spite of the animosity between them spanning a decade, which he now regretted?

APART FROM FEELING most like herself in the studio, Nikki admittedly used it as a way to mask the strong physical awareness she unexpectedly had for Gavin Lynley's presence. Was it wrong to have romantic vibes for someone who hated her for allowing Brigette to talk her into going out that fateful night ten years ago? Was it just as wrong for Gavin to believe that Brigette walked on water as the love of his life—when in reality, she was anything but the faithful girlfriend with eyes only for him?

Telling him now would only make it seem like I'm rewriting history in knocking Brigette off her pedestal when she's no longer alive to defend herself, Nikki mused sadly as she glanced about the art studio. With natural light coming in from a large picture window, there were canvases in various stages of completion on long wooden tables and lining the walls on the floor, along with pencils, brushes and multiple colors of paint ready to use. She liked to move back and forth between projects, tackling one or another whenever the spirit moved her. Aside from when she needed to prioritize for commissioned artworks. Or showings. She imagined painting Gavin, seeing him as the perfect human subject with his handsome, defined features and strong jawline. But his assignment would likely be over practically before it started—ending that fantasy where it probably belonged. In her head and now her heart.

The fact that she'd secretly had feelings for Brigette's boyfriend years ago but had wisely kept them to herself, not wanting to betray her best friend, did not change the reality that there was little chance that anything could happen now between Nikki and Gavin. Apart from the strained relations between them, she had no reason to believe he would ever be interested in her romantically. For all she knew, he was in a serious relationship—if not a marriage—with someone else, now that Brigette, his presumably first true love, was no longer around to give him the family Brigette had indicated he wanted someday. Never mind that Brigette didn't necessarily share his vision for her own future.

I won't open up a can of worms for someone who is merely here on assignment as a special agent, Nikki told herself as she headed to a canvas on an easel that she had started working on. It was a painting of Mississippi wildflowers. It was best not to go there and allow Brigette to rest in peace and Gavin to keep her memory in any way he saw fit. Just as Nikki chose to do, knowing that Brigette would always hold a special place in her heart, flaws and all.

Not to mention that no matter who was responsible for their going out that night, it was Brigette who made the ultimate sacrifice. Even if that was never her intention. While Nikki had somehow managed to escape her own date with death, though not for lack of Perry Evigan's wanting to see her suffer too, through a sexual violation, followed by ligature strangulation.

And now, she feared, he may still come after her, just as he promised, to deal her the same fatal blow he dealt Brigette and nine other women—all with the better part of their lives still ahead of them. Until that was no longer the case.

Nikki could only hope that Gavin was as committed

to preventing this as he appeared to be, their issues notwithstanding. Or that Perry Evigan was captured and put back behind bars, long before he could ever make his way to Owl's Bay.

GAVIN POKED HIS head into the art studio, where he had given Nikki a few uninterrupted hours to work and process the circumstances that brought them together again so suddenly. She was standing before a canvas, painting, and seemingly totally in focus. That didn't mean she had all but forgotten he was there. He was certain that she was just as ill at ease about it as he was. But no matter the second-guessing about the events that led to Brigette's death, it was necessary for him to occupy Nikki's space, as her safety was front and center. Not only as a matter of his directive as a special agent of the Mississippi Department of Corrections CID, but also on a personal level. Gavin hadn't been able to save Brigette from that monster. He would be damned if he allowed Evigan to harm her best friend as well.

He stepped inside the studio and said, to catch her attention, "Hey."

Nikki stopped painting the still life of wildflowers and turned to face him. "Hey." She flashed a tentative expression. "Any news on Perry Evigan?"

Gavin only wished he could tell her that Evigan and his fellow prison escapees had been recaptured and were no longer a danger to the public. Or her, in particular, where it concerned the serial killer. "I'm afraid that Evigan is still on the loose," he told her frustratingly.

She wrinkled her nose. "How have they been able to

avoid capture? I assume law enforcement is on full alert on the prison escape?"

"They are," Gavin assured her. "Trust me, we're doing everything we can to find the escapees. How have they avoided capture?" He waited a beat while moving closer to her. "We're talking about hardened criminals here. They may well have planned their escape long before it actually happened and developed a strategy for staying hidden or otherwise circumventing the law. On the other hand, Evigan and his cronies may simply have gotten lucky, thus far, in evading the authorities. Either way, a BOLO has been issued for the trio, who are believed to still be together, along with the stolen vehicle they may be driving. It's only a matter of time before they're apprehended."

Nikki rolled her eyes. "Why doesn't that give me much comfort?"

"Probably for the same reason it doesn't me," Gavin told her in all honesty. "With Evigan's murderous track record—and Aaron Machado and Craig Schneider aren't any better, as they're also convicted murderers—we can't afford to let our guard down till Evigan's back behind bars."

"No, we definitely can't." A look of apprehension flashed across her face. "So, what now?"

"I stick around for as long as it takes while the man who attacked you and Brigette remains a fugitive." Gavin jutted his chin. "If that's all right with you—?"

Nikki nodded thoughtfully. "It has to be," she said in no uncertain terms. "I just want this over so I can get on with my life without needing to look over my shoulder."

Or having to deal with me and our shared and tragic history, Gavin mused. "I understand." He resisted the urge to touch Nikki's face, imagining how soft it would feel to his fingertips. "If you're hungry, how about we do takeout? It's probably best not to go to a restaurant at night right now," he indicated, knowing that exposing themselves under the cover of darkness could well be playing right into Evigan's hands, assuming he was able to continue to dodge the dragnet.

"Actually, I'm starving," Nikki said. "And, yes, takeout is good. And quicker than cooking something, as I wasn't, umm…prepared for a guest. Short of day-old apple pie."

Gavin grinned sideways. "I had a piece," he told her. "It was tasty."

"Glad you liked it." She showed her teeth, which brightened her good looks that much more. "Brigette taught me how to make one. Before then, I was pretty useless when it came to desserts."

He remembered Brigette being good with apple, cherry and pecan pies—and even chocolate and caramel cake—having been taught the art of making delicious desserts from her own mother. It was one of the things that attracted Gavin to Brigette, given his sweet tooth and all. If only he didn't have to work that fateful night, forcing him to cancel their date. Then Brigette would still be alive and neither she nor Nikki would have ever been victimized by the likes of Perry Evigan.

This was something Gavin would have to live with. Even if he wished Nikki had been stronger in pushing back against Brigette's greater risk-taking ventures.

THE ESCAPED CONS traveled down the back road in the stolen Chrysler Pacifica. They were armed, antsy, hungry and looking for a way to keep the journey to freedom going for as long as possible. In fact, none of them relished the thought of going back to prison. On the contrary, each was willing to do whatever was necessary to avoid doing just that. Having managed to circumvent their pursuers only emboldened them to continue fleeing from them and let the chips fall where they may.

If that meant taking out anyone who stood in their way, then so be it. With nothing to lose, all options were on the table. That included taking hostages and making sure that any and all of their demands were met. Or else.

At least one of the escapees thought that Mexico might be a good option. It would be relatively easy to disappear once there and start over in some small town where each person's business was his own.

Another saw that as a stupid idea, knowing from experience that living south of the border with the authorities in full pursuit would be no walk in the park. Just the opposite. For his part, he would rather remain on the lam in the United States, moving from state to state if necessary. There were plenty of places to hide where one might never be found. Staying one step or two ahead of the law might be challenging, but possible with determination and ingenuity.

The other escapee and self-appointed leader of the group, Perry Evigan, had his own agenda, but kept it to himself. No need to ruffle any feathers at this point when not in a position to speak his mind in a way that would not potentially blow up in his face.

Sitting in the front passenger seat, he gripped tightly the Glock G43X subcompact semiauto pistol in his hands. He saw it as not only protection, but also a means to an end for his desire to achieve his objectives in picking up right where he left off a decade ago as the Gulfport Nightmare Killer.

The one who got away had haunted his dreams, and only she could allow him to be himself again. He wanted that—*her*—more than anything. But before he could even seriously begin to think in those terms, Perry knew he had to figure out a way to survive, with the walls closing in on them, he sensed.

He hadn't come this far in his quest only to be denied. Not when his quarry was out there, waiting for him, more or less.

The pretty face of Nikki Sullivan filled his head. He couldn't help but crack a grin at the thought of her. If he had his way, Perry was sure they would meet again. But the forces working against him could prevent that from ever happening.

Or not.

Chapter Three

In the dining area, Gavin sat in an upholstered side chair across a pedestal table from Nikki and decided it was time to address the elephant in the room. At least this was what he sensed during the mostly quiet and clearly strained eating of their take-out dinner consisting of country-fried steak, mashed potatoes and garden salad, along with coffee. Gazing at her, he said in an earnest tone, "Look, I think we need to clear the air..."

Nikki stopped eating, staring back at him. "The air in here is pretty clear, last time I checked," she spoke wryly.

"I'm sure you know what I mean." Or was this trip down memory lane only one-sided?

She dabbed a paper napkin to her mouth and said thoughtfully, "Well, go on, say what's on your mind."

Gavin took a breath and put down his fork, before responding apologetically, "I shouldn't have taken my frustrations about what happened to Brigette out on you."

"But you did," Nikki said with an edge to her tone. "For the past ten years, you gave me a guilt complex—made me believe that I somehow should've stopped Brigette from wanting to go out. As if." Nikki rolled her eyes at the absurdity of it, with them both knowing just how headstrong Brigette could be when she made up her mind to do something. "And that I was responsible for putting us in harm's way—or the crosshairs of a serial killer—by not insisting that she stay put on a Saturday night after you bailed on her. So, why the change of heart now?" she challenged him.

His shoulders slumped as Gavin was forced to look squarely at his own culpability in not only Brigette's death, but Nikki's suffering at the hands of Perry Evigan. Not to mention being present when he killed her best friend. "You're not going to make this easy for me, are you?"

"Nope." Nikki gave him a firm expression. "Did you want me to?"

"I guess not," he answered, knowing full well that going light on him would only be a cop-out. Which he didn't deserve. Gavin collected his thoughts and said, "The truth of the matter is, on some level—actually, more than that—I've always known that you weren't to blame for what happened to you and Brigette. You were twenty-three-year-olds, just wanting to do what most young people liked to do on a Saturday night—go out and have fun. Neither of you could have anticipated that you would run into Evigan at a club. Or that he would spike your drinks and victimize you further."

Gavin picked up his fork and moved the salad around, as his own guilt took center stage. "If anyone deserves blame for what you were put through—besides the creep who perpetrated the attack—it's me. I've kicked myself more than once over the years, wishing I'd not canceled the date with Brigette. At the time, I was still getting my feet wet on the job and didn't feel I could afford to slack off when duty called. Had I stuck with getting together with Brigette, it probably would've saved her life and spared you what Evigan put you through."

"You can't know that for sure," Nikki countered and lifted her mug of coffee. "Even if Brigette and I hadn't gone out that night, we could have still ended up being targeted by Perry Evigan another night. Maybe that's how the universe works. Fate. Or whatever. Point is, there may have been nothing you or I could have done to prevent what happened—no matter how many times we replayed the what-ifs to try and rewrite history. Or at least reimagined it."

"You're right," Gavin said, somewhat surprised that she had come to his defense, after he had wanted to assuage his own feelings of guilt by putting it on her, to one degree or another. He could only wonder how their friendship would have evolved had they been on the same page years ago in putting the tragedy behind them. "It does no good to rehash everything that went wrong that night. But I'm still sorry that it took me so long to come to this place."

"Me too." She favored him with a tender smile, sipping the coffee. "I know that Brigette—as the person who brought us together—would have wanted us to at least remain friends over the years. So, better late than never, I suppose."

"Yeah, agreed." He grinned at her, believing that having Nikki in his life, even from a distance, was something he needed. The fact that she seemed to feel the same was just as pleasing.

They resumed eating and Gavin considered that the one positive that came from the ordeal was that Evigan was stopped in his tracks—preventing him from victimizing others down the line. That was something to take solace in.

Except for the fact that the serial killer had escaped

from prison. And was still on the loose. Meaning that Nikki was in danger for as long as Evigan remained free.

NIKKI COULD HARDLY believe that she and Gavin had just had a heart-to-heart discussion in confronting the albatross that seemed to hang around their necks for the better part of a decade. She could only imagine Brigette scolding them both for taking so long to bridge the gap as two people important in her life, to one degree or another.

In the process, Nikki realized she'd had to come to terms with the fact that, on some level, she had blamed Gavin for her own victimization. Had he chosen Brigette instead of his job that night, Nikki would have likely stayed home, even if bored out of her mind—thereby sparing her from being almost raped and strangled to death by Perry Evigan. She realized now how foolish that was to think. Gavin had a right to reschedule his date with Brigette to work, not knowing what would go down by virtue of this. He was no more guilty of being responsible for what happened than Nikki was in not trying to talk Brigette out of going out on the town for drinking and dancing.

Agreeing on this was definitely a good thing, Nikki told herself, as she cleared the table with Gavin's help. She welcomed the opportunity to come away as friends, after the dust resettled with Perry Evigan once again behind bars. Or dead, if he resisted arrest.

They sat back at the table with a slice of apple pie for dessert and a glass of red wine. After a few minutes of keeping things light, Nikki decided to be brave and asked Gavin out of curiosity, "So, are you seeing anyone these days?" She hoped she wasn't being too forward, prying into his personal life. But they were on friendly terms again, right?

"No," he responded over his wineglass and without prelude. "I've dated off and on over the years, but nothing stuck."

"I guess Brigette was a hard act to follow, huh?" Nikki said, a twinge of envy coursing through her, knowing that her late friend's feelings weren't entirely reciprocated toward him.

Gavin kept a straight face as he sipped wine and answered coolly, "I did care about Brigette a lot, but I moved on, having no choice but to do so. As for her being a hard act to follow, she was certainly a handful at times as a girlfriend. The truth is, I'm not sure where things were headed between us. Maybe nowhere over the course of time. Regarding being single right now, I guess I'm still waiting for the right person to come along and see what happens—"

"I see." She tasted the wine, while wondering just how long it would take for that right person to come along. Or was he just as picky as she was?

"What about you?" Gavin caught her attention. "Anyone in your life these days?"

"Can't say there is," she told him honestly. "Like you, I've dated people from time to time since moving to Owl's Bay—including, most recently, a guy named Kenan Fernández, a personal trainer—and struck out, unfortunately, insofar as finding my soul mate, if you believe in that type of thing."

"Actually, I do believe it to be true," Gavin surprised her by saying. "When it happens, you just know it."

"Perhaps you're right." She wondered if he thought of

Brigette as his soul mate when they were together. And, if so, would any other woman ever measure up?

He used his fork to cut into the slice of apple pie and said, "So, do you have family? I seem to recall from Brigette that you grew up in what, Clarksdale?"

"Yes, I did." Nikki smiled. "My mother and stepdad still live there. I lost my dad when I was five. I'm an only child. How about you?" Didn't Brigette once mention to her that he had a younger sister?

"I have a sister, Lauren, two years my junior," Gavin confirmed. "She and her husband, Rory, live with their two cute little girls, Ellen and Miley, in Cape Cod. My parents passed away a few years ago, though separately," he said sadly.

"Sorry to hear that." Nikki considered Gavin's pain with having to deal with their losses coming after Brigette's death. Had that also destroyed any plans to have children of his own someday?

"Both had been dealing with some health issues off and on," he noted, "and went pretty quickly at the end. Apart from Lauren and Rory, I had a lot of support in dealing with it from cousins that I'm close to. They all happen to also be gainfully employed in law enforcement careers."

"I remember Brigette mentioning something about that." Nikki tasted the pie thoughtfully. "I'm sure they probably have something to say about the brazen prison escape by Perry Evigan and the others."

"Yeah, whether I want to hear it or not," Gavin quipped. "Seriously, they've got my back and definitely want to see Evigan behind bars again where he belongs."

She sipped her wine musingly. "Where do you think he is right now?"

Gavin put the wineglass to his mouth and then said bluntly, "Running scared and wondering just how much time he has left before his taste of freedom comes crashing down like a house of cards—one way or another..."

Nikki took solace in that assessment, while feeling even greater comfort in Gavin's presence as the last line of defense should Perry Evigan someway, somehow, still show up at her door. Only to have a second crack at her.

BRUSHING SHOULDERS AS they removed the dessert dishes and wineglasses, Gavin once again felt a spark when touching Nikki. Surely, she felt it too? Was there something between them that he had missed a decade ago? Had he hedged his bet wrong when turning his attention to Brigette, when Nikki was just as attractive? And perhaps a better fit for him, character-wise?

"If it's okay with you," Gavin asked Nikki evenly, "I'd like to camp out on your living room sofa for the night—while Evigan is still at large. Or, if that's cramping your style too much, I can sleep out in my car. Not a problem."

"Don't be silly." She dismissed that last notion with a wave of her hand. "No need to spend the night in your vehicle, Special Agent Lynley, in keeping me safe from a dangerous man. Or, for that matter, sleeping on my sofa. It's comfortable, but only to a point." Nikki smiled at him. "As it is, I have a guest room upstairs that you're welcome to stay in, as long as needed. It has an en suite as well, if you want to shower or anything."

"Thanks. I'll take you up on that." Gavin grinned while also feeling an underpinning of desire as he imagined her in bed in another room not far from the spare bedroom—and him in it with her. "I'll just step outside to get my bag."

As he did just that, Gavin scanned the perimeter, looking for any sign of Evigan, while keeping a hand close to the 9mm semiautomatic pistol in his holster. He saw nothing out of the ordinary or otherwise suspicious and so Gavin continued on to his Chevrolet Tahoe. *If Evigan dares to show up here, I'll arrest him and he'll be back in prison where he belongs in no time flat*, Gavin told himself, while grabbing his tote bag and heading back inside the house.

"I set some fresh towels on the bed," Nikki told him.

"Appreciate that." He smiled and they both climbed the stairwell and Gavin was led to the guest room.

"Here you go," she pointed out.

Gavin glanced inside the room and saw rustic furniture, including a log bed. He thanked her again for the hospitality. "This will do just fine," he said nicely.

Nikki gave a nod. "If you need anything, let me know."

"Will do."

"Good night."

"Good night," he told her, watching briefly as she walked away, while wondering how he could have wasted a decade blaming her for something that was entirely on Perry Evigan. And no one else. At least Nikki didn't seem to hold it against him after they had talked this through. Gavin saw that as a positive step forward for both of them.

After closing the door, he removed his firearm, setting it on the wicker nightstand, along with his holster. Then Gavin pulled out his cell phone and fell onto a rattan armchair, where he reached out to the Owl's Bay Police Department to make sure they were on the same page in terms of the BOLO for Perry Evigan and the other escapees. That seemed to be the case, which gave Gavin comfort, wanting there to be as many sets of eyes keeping watch in town for the prisoners as possible. Even if it appeared to be a long shot at face value that the trio would show up in Owl's Bay as a group. Gavin only wished he could feel as confident where it concerned Evigan operating alone, still envisioning the serial killer's smug face after his arrest, during the trial and upon his conviction. It was obvious that Nikki remembered this too.

Gavin called his cousin, Scott Lynley, returning a voice mail he'd left earlier. An FBI special agent and cold case specialist, working at the field office in Louisville, Kentucky, he and Scott, who was a few years older, were always cool and supportive of each other's careers and personal trials and tribulations.

Scott answered the video chat request, his oblong face appearing on the screen. "Hey."

Gavin gazed at Scott, who had gray eyes and thick black hair in a comb-over pomp, low-fade style. "Hey."

"I heard about Perry Evigan's daring escape from prison."

"Who hasn't by now?" Gavin pursed his lips.

Scott furrowed his brow. "Are they any closer to catching him?"

"I'd sure as hell like to think so," he told him. "But as of now, Evigan and his prison buddies, Aaron Machado and Craig Schneider, are still roaming free."

"That's too bad."

"Tell me about it." Gavin sighed, jutting his chin.

"No doubt your old girlfriend, Brigette, and the other women Evigan murdered are spinning in their graves, wondering how this could have happened."

"They seized on the distraction from the uprising,"

Gavin muttered. "Which shows there's still a major flaw in the system that the three were able to pull it off."

"They won't get very far," Scott said. "The FBI is doing its part to help track them down as soon as possible."

Gavin nodded. "I know and am grateful for the support."

Scott paused. "Have you contacted the surviving victim of Evigan? I know you had your differences…"

"Nikki's been alerted about the escape and is safe," Gavin reported. "I've been assigned to stick with her till Evigan is back in custody."

"Really?" Scott cocked a brow. "How's that working out?"

"Better than expected." He sat back thoughtfully. "We're good," he told him. "Or at least have found a better way to deal with Brigette's death without pointing fingers."

"That's good to hear."

"Yeah." Gavin listened as Scott briefly talked about his own latest investigation and recent second marriage, before they disconnected.

After taking a shower, Gavin hit the sack, falling asleep, while thinking about Nikki.

An hour later, he awakened to the sound of a woman screaming.

Nikki. She was in danger.

Jumping out of bed, wearing only knit pajama shorts, Gavin sprang into action. He grabbed his pistol off the nightstand and ran out of the room and down the hall toward Nikki's bedroom.

Stepping inside, Gavin expected to see Perry Evigan looming over Nikki, in the process of trying to strangle her. At which point, he would stop the serial killer escapee by any means necessary.

Instead, Gavin was quickly able to establish that Nikki was in the room by herself, restless on the platform bed from what appeared to be a bad dream. Evigan had not managed to disengage the security system and enter the house with murder on his mind.

Moving past traditional furnishings to the bed, where Nikki was squirming and moaning beneath a patchwork bedspread, Gavin sat on it and grabbed her gently by the shoulders and jostled her awake as he called out her name.

"Get off me!" Nikki shrieked, as she flailed at him as if he was attacking her. She half sat up and out of the bedding, wearing a red chemise lingerie nightgown.

"Nikki, it's Gavin," he said gently, blocking her attempts to strike him in the face.

"Gavin?" Nikki opened her eyes and settled down upon gazing at him. "What are you doing in my bedroom?"

"I heard you scream," Gavin explained, releasing her. "I thought you were in serious trouble. But it looks like you were just having a bad dream."

"Oh." Her tone quieted.

"You're safe."

"I remember now," she said, ill at ease. "I was dreaming that Perry Evigan was trying to…well, do everything he wanted to do before—" She drew a breath. "Thank goodness it was all in my head."

"Do you often have nightmares about him?" Gavin wondered, feeling bad that she'd even had one.

"I used to. Especially in the years right after it happened. Not so much lately." Nikki looked up at him.

"Guess the fact that Evigan escaped triggered a return to the nightmares. Sorry if I woke you up."

"No apologies necessary," Gavin stressed. "I'm sorry that Evigan being on the loose triggered the bad dream. Hopefully, the dream and his freedom will be short-lived."

"I hope so too."

"Try to go back to sleep." Gavin felt a strong need to protect her at all costs. "I'll be just down the hall, if you need me."

"All right." Nikki touched his hand. "Thank you for coming to my rescue. Even if it turned out that I didn't really need rescuing in this instance."

"Actually, I think you did," he begged to differ. "Nightmares can be just as frightening as real life. I wouldn't have sat back and allowed you to be victimized again by Evigan, even within your subconscious mind."

Against his desire of wanting to stay the night in her room to make Nikki feel more secure, Gavin left and went back to his own room, knowing that the longer Evigan remained out of prison, the more he would be able to wreak havoc on Nikki's psyche, along with his own.

Chapter Four

"Were you able to get back to sleep last night?" Gavin asked as they ate breakfast the following morning.

"Yes, surprisingly," Nikki told him across the table, where she spooned cereal, to go with toast and coffee, while fully dressed. She had figured that, after the nightmare, she would stay awake all night, freaking out over the likes of Perry Evigan. But perhaps knowing that Gavin was just down the hall and committed to keeping her from harm made the difference. "How about you?" She hoped he said yes, hating to think that his guard duty included pulling all-nighters.

"Yeah, I pretty much slept like a baby," he claimed with a straight face. He added, "But kept one eye open, just in case."

She chuckled. "That must have been challenging."

"Not so much." He grinned. "Comes with the territory sometimes."

Nikki colored. "You mean you jar awake other witnesses or victims having nightmares, as a routine thing?"

"Not really." Gavin laughed and bit into a piece of toast. "But in this business, you have to be ready for everything. Including needing to get out of bed at a moment's notice in the wee hours of the morning."

She tasted the coffee and, eyeing him, asked curiously, "So, where do you live when you're not on bodyguard duty?"

"I'm based in Jackson," he said matter-of-factly.

"I see." She lifted her spoon. "I've visited Jackson a few times. There's a thriving art scene there."

"Really?" Gavin titled his face as though totally shocked. "Can't say I've been much into the art world—I'm more of a college-football-and spy-novels–type guy—but after seeing some of what you bring to the table, I'm becoming a true fan of your works."

Nikki blushed. "That's sweet of you to say." She would gladly invite him to her showing next week, but assumed he would be long gone by then. The notion of such was already depressing, even though it would also mean, presumably, that Perry Evigan had been captured. But then again, wasn't that why Gavin showed up at her house in the first place? No one said anything about him extending his time there. Much less moving beyond that by getting to know one another better. "Speaking of art," she said, shifting thoughts, "I need to step out for some supplies this morning." She assumed she wouldn't need to put her entire life on hold while Evigan was out there somewhere as a free man.

"No problem," Gavin spoke smoothly. He sipped coffee. "I'll drive you."

"Okay," she agreed, and bit into a piece of toast.

Shortly, they were in his vehicle and Nikki was still trying to come to grips with the fact that they were sharing the same space and no longer at each other's throats. She could only imagine what Brigette might think if she could see them now. Would she encourage them to cultivate their newfound camaraderie after years of animosity that centered squarely around her? Be jealous that there seemed to be a romantic connection of sorts forming between them? Or might Brigette have actually felt relieved that she could be single again and pursue someone other than Gavin, who might be more suited for her style and character?

"Have you always known you wanted to be an artist?" He intruded upon Nikki's thoughts.

"I suppose I have," she admitted, "ever since I was a little girl and spent much of my spare time with crayons and coloring books with all types of interesting pictures that I envisioned drawing or painting from scratch."

"Looks as though your instincts and talents have paid off for you."

"I do all right for myself," Nikki uttered modestly.

Gavin grinned. "Yeah, I think you have, and more."

"How did you end up working for the Mississippi Department of Corrections anyway?" She looked at him curiously. "As opposed to the FBI, DEA, Homeland Security, or a local police department?"

"It's a good question," he said, switching lanes as they approached an intersection. "Well, while I was a senior majoring in criminology at Mississippi State, their Career Center helped me land a job with the MDOC. I went with it—in separating myself from an uncle and cousins in law enforcement—and have been at this ever since. Overall, it's been worthwhile helping to deal with inmate issues inside and outside the penitentiary, as well as investigations involving corrections personnel who cross the line. Then there's special assignments, such as protecting crime victims or witnesses."

"Like me?" Nikki smiled at him.

"Yeah, exactly." Gavin glanced at her. "In this instance, there was the added incentive of not wanting to see history repeat itself."

"Definitely wouldn't want that," she had to agree, while feeling maudlin thinking about what happened to Brigette—even more than what Nikki went through herself—in destroying her friend's life. And any chance she might have had of happiness, with or without Gavin.

GAVIN PULLED INTO the parking lot of the Owl's Bay Art Shop on Quail Street. As they got out of the car and headed for the store, he was keen on checking out the surroundings. There had been no sightings this morning, thus far, of the escapees. Least of all, Perry Evigan. Gavin had no reason to believe he had come to town, but kept a lookout for him nonetheless and remained armed to that effect.

Once inside, he took a sweeping glance at the main area with art supplies, then looked into two aisles with various arts and crafts, before deciding it was safe for Nikki to go about her business. Gavin watched as she grabbed a basket and said to him, "This shouldn't take long."

"Take your time," he said evenly, knowing he was committed to her well-being, wherever she happened to be while Evigan continued to circumvent the authorities. When his cell phone rang, Gavin removed it from the back pocket of his twill pants and saw that the caller was Special Agent Jean O'Reilly. Probably miffed that he left her hanging. Or appeared to. "I need to get this," he told Nikki.

"Please do." She offered him a grin. "I think I can manage on my own for a while."

He smiled. "All right."

Walking away, Gavin stepped outside, passing a shorter, solid-in-build Hispanic male in his forties, with shoulder-length brown hair parted on the side, who was entering the art shop. He was wearing workout clothes and white sneakers. His dark eyes met briefly with Gavin's, before looking away.

Gavin waited until the man had gone into the building before taking a few steps and accepting the video chat request. He watched Agent O'Reilly's face appear on the screen. "Hey."

"You might have given me a heads-up that you'd been reassigned, Lynley," she snapped.

"I had to leave on short notice," he said by way of apology. "Besides, technically speaking, I haven't exactly been reassigned, per se." He glanced at the art store window. "I'm sure you've heard about the prison break?"

"Of course. And Director Whitfield filled me in on your assignment of protecting serial killer escapee, Perry Evigan's former victim, while he remains on the prowl. I just don't get why it had to be you—with the FBI and US Marshals fully capable of keeping her safe."

"Maybe the director failed to mention that the victim, Nikki Sullivan, was the best friend of my then-girlfriend, Brigette Fontana—who was one of the ten women murdered by Evigan." Gavin wrinkled his nose, still feeling guilty for not being around to protect Brigette from him. Or Nikki, for that matter. "Nikki barely survived the ordeal herself. Anyway, between the two, it gave me added incentive to accept the assignment, along with the fact that it will be of short duration, in all likelihood—meaning that I should be back in Jackson in no time flat to continue mop-up work on the Titus Malfoy investigation."

"I didn't realize you had a personal connection to Evigan's crimes." Jean's face reddened. "Sorry about your ex—and for coming down on you."

"Don't give it a second thought," Gavin said. "I should have called you and explained why I had to leave town abruptly."

"So, how's Ms. Sullivan holding up?"

"Not that well, considering," he responded in all honesty. "Last night, she woke up screaming from a bad dream about Evigan."

Jean frowned. "That's understandable, given what he put her through."

"True." Gavin gazed again at the store, while wondering just how many supplies Nikki needed to buy. "She's better today. But of course, until we can get Perry Evigan and the other escapees back into custody, Nikki's likely to have more restless days and nights."

"Their taste of freedom won't last long," she reassured him. "We've got people searching everywhere and anywhere the prisoners were allegedly spotted—or may have gone or be en route toward. Needless to say, the Mississippi Department of Corrections has some major egg on its face for allowing this escape to take place. As such, we're pulling out all the stops to make up for it—hopefully, before the inmates can hurt anyone else."

"Good to know," Gavin told her, still feeling anxious till it was a done deal.

"If you need any backup there, let me know," Jean said. "I'm sure the case against Titus Malfoy can wait, especially now that he's been arrested."

"I've got it covered, for now, with the locals on full alert."

"All right."

"I have to go," he told her, wanting to get back inside, in case Nikki needed help carrying out her supplies. "See you when I see you."

"Ditto," she said.

Gavin closed down the conversation and glanced around, before heading toward the door of the art store.

"WHAT ARE YOU doing here?" Nikki asked, wide-eyed, as she stared Kenan Fernández in the face.

The personal trainer, whom she had made the mistake of going out to lunch with a week and a half ago, after meeting at an Owl's Bay fitness club, narrowed his eyes and said in a perturbed tone of voice, "Why haven't you returned my calls and text messages?"

She shuddered, sensing the hostility in him as someone who apparently didn't take rejection very well. "I thought I'd made it perfectly clear that I wasn't interested in anything further with you, Kenan," she spoke sharply, glancing over his shoulder for any sign of Gavin. "Responding to the calls and texts would only have encouraged—or upset—you. I didn't want either."

He lowered his chin. "Maybe if you just give us another chance, it can work out between us," he pleaded.

"I don't think so." She regarded him warily. "How did you know I was here?"

"I didn't," Kenan claimed, peering back at her. "I just happened to see you through the window when passing by."

"I don't believe you," Nikki said straightforwardly, switching the basket she was carrying from one hand to the other. She didn't believe in these types of random encounters. Not even in a relatively small town.

"It's the truth." Then, abruptly, he reversed the denial. "Okay, so I followed you from your place."

"You what?" She flashed him a hot stare while contemplating his chilling words. How did he know where she lived? "You're stalking me?"

"Not exactly." Kenan shuffled his feet. "When you never answered my calls or texts, I had my ways of discovering where you stayed and went there this morning—hoping we could talk. Then I saw you leaving with some dude. Who the hell is he to you…?"

As Nikki fumbled with a response, while considering the question at face value, recognizing the metamorphosis of her relationship to Gavin, she read the irrational jealousy in Kenan's glare. What gave him the right to pry into her personal life after one meaningless date?

Before an answer to his demand escaped her lips, Gavin walked up to them and looked from one to the other, then asked in a commanding voice, "Is there a problem?"

"Not unless he chooses to make it one," she answered tensely, and faced her stalker. "I think Kenan was just leaving. Isn't that right?" Nikki challenged him to say otherwise as he and Gavin stood toe to toe.

Gavin, taller and clearly the more intimidating of the two men, added more fuel to the fire in putting Kenan on notice, by saying boldly, "She's with me. Or I'm with her, whichever you prefer. I'd leave it at that, if I were you."

While Kenan seemed to be considering his options, Nikki was struck by Gavin's characterization of their *being together*. Though she was sure that it was meant more to send Kenan a message that she was unavailable in romantic terms than in Gavin's official capacity as her protector from Perry Evigan—Nikki almost found herself wishing that the former was true. Even if it may have been unreasonable to wish for, given their stressed history and association with Brigette.

Abruptly, Kenan made a noise that sounded like growling, eyeing Nikki sharply once more, and walking off like a defeated man.

She and Gavin waited till he was out of listening distance, after which Gavin said observantly, "So, what was that all about? I only caught enough of the conversation to gather that the man wasn't welcome company."

"He definitely was not," Nikki confirmed without prelude, as she suddenly felt the weight of her loaded basket. "That was Kenan Fernández, the personal trainer I mentioned going out with once. He followed us here from my house, wherever he got the address from. Looks like he doesn't know how to take no for an answer, even when calls and texts have gone unanswered."

Gavin frowned. "Sounds like the classic stalker. If you think he failed to get the message loud and clear, I can have a talk with him. Or make a call to local law enforcement about him..."

"Thanks, but neither should be necessary at the moment," she told him, though Nikki welcomed Gavin's coming to her aid outside his mandate. "I don't want to blow this out of proportion. Whatever his problem is, I doubt that he wants the police on his case," she stressed. "Hopefully, this will be the last I'll ever hear from him."

"Hopefully. But should that change while I'm still around, let me know," Gavin told her, an edge to his tone. "In my experience of dealing with inmates who were involved in intimate violence that included stalking and worse, this oftentimes escalated into more stalking and other criminal behavior."

"Hmm…" Nikki furrowed her brow, clearly uncomfortable. "Not exactly what I need at this time in my life—with Perry Evigan still on the loose," she admitted.

"I know. Just keep your guard up," Gavin cautioned, running a hand along his firm jawline. "Everything will be fine."

She nodded, taking him at his word. "If you say so."

"Why don't I grab that basket for you," he said, removing it from her hand before she could object, "and we can get out of here—if you have everything you need?"

"I do," she told him, offering a grateful smile. Other than perhaps peace of mind that was certainly reduced when having to deal with a potential stalker and a definite serial killer.

Chapter Five

Nikki was back in her art studio, putting away supplies, feeling like she was in her comfort zone. At least to the extent possible, with a ruthless serial killer potentially targeting her again—Gavin's strong presence in the other room notwithstanding. Beyond that disturbing reality of Perry Evigan still very much on the loose, it really irked her that Kenan Fernández knew where she lived, further encroaching upon the safety net she had established since moving to Owl's Bay. Perhaps she hadn't moved far enough away from Gulfport and the dark memories that had hung over her there like a cumulus cloud.

Could she have ever run far enough away from something that was bound to stay with her for the rest of her life, to one degree or another? Maybe not. But the fortitude that had empowered her over time would need to carry her through the present danger. And even afterward, when Gavin Lynley was no longer around to protect her from the bad guys. As much as Nikki had quickly gotten used to having him around, the man had a life of his own that didn't include her. Or Brigette, for that matter, as Gavin had obviously moved on from their short romance.

It was only brought back to the forefront with the prison escape of Perry Evigan. Would Gavin just as easily be able to put the genie back in the bottle—and Nikki with it—once the serial killer was safely back behind bars? As if their bonding on one or more levels since Gavin had come to town had never occurred?

Being on her own these days had suddenly no longer seemed like the way to go. Nikki truly did want someone in her life. Could Gavin fill that void? Or was the specter of what happened to Brigette anything but water under the bridge?

"Hey," Gavin's voice penetrated her reverie.

Nikki turned to see him standing there, close enough to touch. She had to fight herself not to do that very thing. "Hey."

"Are you all right?"

"I'm fine," she told him with a straight face.

He smiled at her. "We'll get through this—together."

Nikki liked the sound of that: together. "Okay."

"So, what are you working on right now?" Gavin gazed over her shoulder at the painting covered by a sheet and over a canvas drop cloth on the floor. "Or is that a trade secret in your world, till your latest masterpiece is finished?"

"No trade secrets, I'm afraid." She laughed. "Not sure I would call the oil painting a masterpiece, but here it is…" Nikki lifted the sheet to reveal a landscape that showed off Owl's Bay, complete with open land, loblolly pine trees, housing and a snippet of the Jourdan River for good measure. "It's still a work in progress, but I'm just about there, as part of my showing on Saturday." She looked up at him with a curious slant of her eyes. "So, what do you think?"

"I think it's amazing," he responded without preface. "You really know what you're doing in giving art lovers something to work with."

She blushed. "Is that so?"

"Yes, most definitely." He paused, rubbing his chin. "Brigette was always gung-ho on your talent—maybe even jealous in a way. I think she'd be applauding you now."

"Hopefully, she would be applauding us both," Nikki put forth contemplatively. "And we'd be applauding her in return, knowing that, as a go-getter, she would be a big success in whatever she chose to do."

Gavin gave her a thoughtful look. "I agree."

Nikki couldn't help but wonder if the two of them would have ended up together—no matter Brigette's preference for playing the field without Gavin being the wiser. Or would he have realized that they weren't right for each other at the end of the day and given someone else a chance to make him happy?

Nikki regarded Gavin keenly and gave an honest assessment when she put it out there by saying, "It would be great if I could paint you someday." She was sure this was an implausible scenario, given the time limit of his presence in town.

"Me?" Gavin cocked a brow. "Not sure I'd make a very good subject."

"Are you kidding? With your classic features and good looks, you'd make an excellent subject for a portrait."

"Thanks for saying that," he uttered. "I'm flattered."

Nikki toned down her enthusiasm. "Of course, I realize that you won't be around much longer, once Evigan is tracked down and sent back to prison."

"That's true," Gavin admitted. "But that doesn't mean I couldn't come back…to sit for the painting, that is…"

"That would be nice." She smiled at him, while trying hard not to read anything else into the suggestion. Such as wishing to do a return visit to spend more time with her as someone he was interested in seeing again.

I won't put unspoken thoughts into his head, Nikki told herself, even if she found appeal in the notion of extending this new comradery between them beyond his role as her special agent bodyguard.

Gavin's cell phone rang. He lifted it from the back pocket of his pants, gazed at it and said, "I better get this—"

Nikki nodded and watched as he turned away and took the call. "Lynley," he spoke routinely into the phone. His body language and tone of voice while responding to the caller told Nikki that something was up regarding the status of the escaped convicts.

GAVIN WAS TENSE as he listened to the MDOC Director of Investigations, Marvin Whitfield, who said in a heated voice, "There's been a major break in the investigation… We think that Evigan, Machado and Schneider are holed up inside an abandoned farmhouse in St. Clair County, Alabama—"

"Really?" Gavin glanced at Nikki, who was watching him intently, undoubtedly sensing that the call pertained to the prison escapees.

"Yeah, deputies from the St. Clair County Sheriff's Office spotted a black Chrysler Pacifica matching the one the prisoners stole in Boyle, Mississippi," the director said. "They changed the plates, but a neighbor reported seeing three men matching the physical descriptions of the escaped cons running from the car and inside the farmhouse. We were able to determine through the VIN and DMV that the vehicle in question was, in fact, the one belonging to and stolen from Donald Takeuchi, in Boyle."

"So where do things stand now?" Gavin asked anxiously.

"The farmhouse is surrounded by our Fugitive Apprehension Strike Team, US Marshals, FBI agents and the St. Clair County Sheriff's Office's SWAT Team," Whitfield reported. "We also have on hand a Mississippi Department of Public Safety crisis negotiator—with the aim of getting the escapees to give up and end this thing peacefully."

"Any indication that they have hostages inside?" Gavin wondered.

"Not at this time. If that is the case, we'll deal with it."

"Keep me posted on how this goes down," Gavin told him after being briefed a bit more on the logistics of the operation underway.

Once he was off the phone, Nikki moved closer to him and, with eyes narrowed, asked eagerly, "What's happening?"

"It appears that Perry Evigan and the other two escapees are surrounded inside a rural farmhouse in Alabama. They're trying to get them to surrender. That hasn't happened yet."

Nikki breathed a sigh of relief. "As long as the escapees are at least contained, it means Evigan can't get away to come after me—or anyone else," she stressed boldly.

"True." Gavin could see how much the prospect of the serial killer who victimized her being apprehended took a giant load off Nikki's shoulders. He suddenly found himself taking her into his arms for comfort. "It'll be okay," he maintained, feeling her heart beating fast, along with maybe his own. "Evigan is far away from here and has his hands full. He can't hurt you. I'll see to that."

When Nikki lifted her chin and peered into his eyes, Gavin sensed that she wanted him to kiss her as much as he wanted to do just that. He hesitated for a moment, questioning if it was wise to give in to desire, given their history—before tossing caution to the wind for what felt right. He lowered his head and claimed her mouth. The kiss was slow and steady, soft and hard, sizzling with intensity, rattling his bones while they held on to one another.

Gavin caught his breath after pulling back. He didn't want to ruin a good thing. Mislead. Or be misled. "Do you want to go grab a bite to eat?" he asked her. "With the threat of Evigan as a fugitive apparently being neutralized even as we speak, it shouldn't pose much of a risk to dine in a public place."

Nikki nodded as she touched her swollen lips. "All right."

He resisted the urge to touch her while offering a soft smile, even as Gavin wondered where things were headed—or not—for them, when he no longer had an excuse for being in her world once Perry Evigan was again out of the picture.

MARVIN WHITFIELD SAT edgily at his walnut L-shaped corner desk at the Mississippi Department of Corrections Central Office headquarters. His raven eyes flashed between the laptop before him and a picture window that provided a respite from the pressure he felt. As the Director of Investigations in the Corrections Investigation Division, it ultimately fell on him to spearhead the recapture of the escaped prisoners from the Mississippi State Penitentiary. Beyond that, he needed to learn what weaknesses in the system allowed Perry Evigan, Craig Schneider and Aaron Machado to exploit the prison riot to successfully engineer their escape.

Frankly, it drew the ire of Whitfield that this had happened under his watch. It wasn't exactly what he wanted on his résumé when the opportunity to move up the ladder of the MDOC presented itself. He would make damn sure to hold the MSP superintendent, Crystal Rawlings, and warden, Zachary Livingston, accountable for the melee and escape. Including, as a result, the death of correctional officer Stan MacGregor, with another guard, Stewart Siegfried, still listed in critical condition.

Right now, Whitfield was most interested in getting the inmates back behind bars where they belonged. Particularly Perry Evigan. He had been following the investigation into the serial killer's strangulation murders, and Whitfield was elated when they were able to apprehend, convict and incarcerate Evigan. The fact that Gavin Lynley had been involved with Evigan's last homicide victim, Brigette Fontana, and was acquainted with a surviving victim, Nikki Sullivan, made it all the more urgent that they recapture Evigan. Then both Gavin and Nikki could try to put this behind them again and get on with their lives.

At least that was the plan as Whitfield saw it. With Evigan and the other fugitives cornered in the farmhouse, it now seemed only a matter of time before their violent escape came to an end—through one means or another. The director grabbed his cell phone off the desk and called the leader of the FAST at the scene and crisis negotiator for an update.

NIKKI FELT NERVOUS excitement over the prospect of Perry Evigan being arrested again and put back in prison for the rest of his life—facing charges on at least two more homicides to add to his killings. *Who knows how many others he might have strangled to death or otherwise murdered the longer he had remained a free man?* she thought. Still, she was so glad that he and the other fugitives were nowhere near Owl's Bay, forcing her to have to relive a nightmare. Not that she didn't have help warding off danger in Gavin, who was just as affected by the serial killer's being a free man as she was. They both needed this to be over so Brigette could once again be able to rest in peace.

She glanced across the wooden table at the Owl's Bay Country Restaurant on Talridge Avenue, where Gavin was eating pan-seared Atlantic salmon with collard greens, as she had a tuna and butter bean salad. In the moment, Nikki couldn't help but think about kissing him. Or was it the other way around? Whichever—apart from the tickle she felt from her face touching the hair on his chin—the kiss had sent lightning shooting throughout her body like nothing she'd ever felt before. Then, just like that, it was over. Neither of them said a word afterward, as if to do so would imply that it meant something. Or not. She felt confused and had some clarity at the same time, knowing that she was beginning to develop feelings for the man. Even if it was one-sided and destined to go nowhere, all things being equal with their history and separate lives and locations presently.

"About the kiss..." they both voiced at the same time.

"Yeah, that..." Nikki colored, deciding to protect herself by taking the lead. "It was nothing," she suggested. "We were both just caught up in the moment. No worries."

"I was thinking the same thing," Gavin contended, dabbing a paper napkin to a corner of his mouth. "You're a great kisser though," he threw out, as though to lessen the awkwardness of the moment.

"So are you," she had to admit, and forked her salad musingly.

"We're good, then?" He met her eyes coolly, his face tilted to one side.

"We're good." Nikki was happy to leave it at that. Or maybe not, but felt it was for the best. Nothing to be gained by getting in over her head for the special agent whose mission and presence in her life were just about up.

As though to relieve the tenseness of the moment, Gavin asked her, "Aside from being an artist, which obviously can be time-consuming, what else do you like to do for fun or whatever?"

"Well, I teach an art class once a week at the local community college," she told him. "I wouldn't necessarily call it fun, but it's certainly rewarding in helping others learn the proper techniques in their own artistic pursuits." Nikki didn't need to give it much thought beyond that as she said, "On the fun front, I like to go to the gym, play tennis, swim, dance—though no style in particular—and read romance and thriller novels."

"Sounds pretty well-rounded to me."

"I suppose. And how about you?" she asked, lifting her glass of water. "What do you do for fun outside of working as a special agent for the Mississippi Department of Corrections?" Given what great shape he was in, Nikki could already imagine some pastimes.

"I like to work out," he confirmed evenly. "I jog, bicycle, listen to jazz and what else—oh, sing in the shower when no one else is listening." He laughed. "I'm not very good at it."

"Do you still go dancing?" She gazed at him thoughtfully. "I seem to recall that you and Brigette loved to hang out at dance clubs." Nikki tried to put out of her mind that Brigette was just as content to dance with any other guy who asked her when Gavin wasn't around.

"Every now and then," he responded. "Maybe if I had the right dance partner these days..."

Nikki refused to draw anything from that, though she too felt the same way, as she imagined them ballroom dancing together. Or slow dancing, cheek to cheek.

Gavin broke into her reverie when he asked, "Do you like to travel?"

"Yes," she said. "I've been to Mexico, England and Italy, along with typical hot spots in the US, like Las Vegas, Los Angeles, Miami and New York City—all with booming art scenes. I'd love to go on a cruise someday."

"Yeah, a cruise does sound like it could be fun." He sat back, thoughtful. "Can't say I can match that as far as overseas travel, but I have been to a law enforcement conference in Singapore, visited the Bahamas and a couple of places in Canada. Like you, I've made my way around the country, here and there, for both business and leisure—but always find myself back at home in Mississippi."

"Me too." Nikki smiled. Honestly, she had pondered moving elsewhere once or twice. Especially right after the ordeal with Perry Evigan. But she refused to allow him to drive her away from her home state, giving that monster more power over her life.

Gavin's cell phone rang. He met Nikki's eyes and her

heart skipped a beat as she sensed that there was news on the standoff between the escaped cons and the authorities surrounding them.

Chapter Six

"Hey," Special Agent Jean O'Reilly spoke to him over the phone. "Just got word that the standoff is over."

"Really?" Gavin perked up as he gazed across the table to Nikki, who had an equally vested interest in this. He put it on speakerphone. "Tell me more…"

"Well, according to Matt Baccarin from the Fugitive Apprehension Strike Team, there was a shootout between the escaped convicts and our side," she said. "Whether something ignited accidentally or was started deliberately, the farmhouse caught on fire, trapping those inside. They were apparently determined to fight it out till the end—refusing to surrender."

Gavin shifted on the seat and asked, "So, they're all dead…?"

"Yeah, I'm afraid so," Jean confirmed. "Once the fire was put out by members of the St. Clair County Fire and EMS Association, three bodies were removed by the St. Clair County Medical Examiner and Coroner's Office."

"Have they been able to confirm that Perry Evigan is, in fact, one of the deceased individuals?" Gavin had to ask, eyeing Nikki again, knowing this was important for her peace of mind too.

"Not yet," the special agent told him. "The victims of

the fire were burned beyond recognition. Dental records for Evigan, Machado and Schneider will be examined by forensic dentists to positively identify the deceased. Shouldn't take too long to confirm the identities, but all signs point to the dead being the three fugitives—Perry Evigan included."

"Okay," Gavin told her. He added, though knowing that Director Whitfield would fill him in on further details of the investigation, "Thanks for the update and keep me posted on any new developments."

"Will do." Jean sighed. "For what it's worth, if it turns out that Evigan is dead, both you and Nikki Sullivan should be able to breathe a little easier in knowing that the Gulfport Nightmare Killer will no longer be around to terrorize anyone he decides to target or who gets in his way."

"It's worth a lot, Jean," he assured her, and hung up, then identified her to Nikki for the record as Special Agent Jean O'Reilly of the MDOC.

Nodding, Nikki wasted no time in saying with a catch to her voice, "So, it looks like Evigan's evil deeds have finally caught up with him."

"Yeah, looks that way." Gavin gave her a little grin, then turned serious. "We'll know soon enough."

"For all his faults—and they seemed to be endless Perry Evigan is still human," she stressed. "If he was truly inside the farmhouse, I'm pretty sure that he didn't develop wings and somehow fly away to evade capture and continue his evil ways."

"I agree. Evigan's definitely not superhuman. Or an invincible extraterrestrial." Gavin chuckled and ran a fork haphazardly through what was left of his collard greens. "Still, until we get the official word that he truly is dead, if it's all the same to you, I'd like to stick around." Gavin wasn't quite ready to return to Jackson and his own life full-time. Not with the passionate kiss they shared that still resonated with him, in spite of going along with the notion that it was merely a moment of weakness and nothing more. For his part, he wanted to put that theory to the test. If the kiss did mean something, didn't they owe it to themselves to explore this further? Or was his point of view entirely different from hers?

"I would like that," Nikki told him, flashing a nice smile. "What's that old saying about never counting the chickens before the eggs hatch? I think we should continue hanging out till Perry Evigan's death has been verified through forensic dentistry and the coroner, or any other means..."

Gavin grinned. "Then it's settled."

Even as he said the words, though happy to extend his stay at least a little while longer, per his assignment, internally, Gavin wasn't quite sure that was true where it pertained to his growing attraction to Nikki and where it could possibly lead down the road.

"HEY," NIKKI SAID to her mother and stepdad on a laptop video chat, while she sat in an Adirondack chair on the rear deck of her cottage. She had delayed phoning them as long as possible, knowing how freaked out they would be in learning that the man who tried to rape and murder her had broken out of prison and would possibly come after her again. Normally, Nikki might have assumed they had already heard the news. But she knew that the prison escape coincided with their long-awaited vacation to the Cayman Islands in the Caribbean. It was highly unlikely that the news would have traveled there, nor would she have wanted this to cast a shadow on their holiday. But now it didn't have to, with what she could tell them.

"Hi, honey," Nikki's mother said, a bright smile lighting up her pretty face. A retired middle school teacher, Dorothy McElligott was in her sixties, slender, blue-eyed behind horn-shaped glasses, and had blondish-silver hair worn in a pixie cut.

"Hey, there," William McElligott said, sitting beside her on a black leather sofa in their hotel room. Also in his sixties, big and strong, with slicked-back salt-and-pepper short hair, a hipster beard and gray-brown eyes, Nikki had always considered the pharmacist her mother married more than two decades ago to be her father, while barely remembering her real dad.

"How are you enjoying the Cayman Islands?" she asked them cheerfully.

"It's everything we thought it would be—and so much more," her mother gushed.

"Wish you could have joined us," William pitched in.

"Me too," Nikki said sincerely. "Maybe next time." She waited a beat before saying, "I have to tell you something—"

Dorothy's brows lowered, showing concern. "What is it?"

Nikki drew a breath and said, "Two days ago, Perry Evigan broke out of prison…"

"What?" Her mother cringed. "How?"

"He and two other violent prisoners managed to escape during a prison riot," she reported to them.

"And we're just finding out about this now?" William's thick brows knitted.

"I didn't want to worry you guys," Nikki explained, "putting a damper on your trip."

"We're your parents," Dorothy snapped. "It's our job to worry—no matter how old you are."

"She speaks for me too," her stepdad said earnestly.

"I'm sorry." Nikki almost felt as though she were living back at home under their protective thumbs again, but understood why they would be upset. "Anyway, the good news is that it appears Evigan and the other escapees were trapped in an Alabama farmhouse that caught on fire—killing all three."

"Well, that's a relief," her mother said, her features relaxing a bit, "even if you never want anyone to die that way."

William wasn't quite as magnanimous when he said bluntly, "When you break out of a penitentiary, whatever happens afterward is on you."

"Dental records will be used to positively identify the remains," Nikki told them. "But the authorities believe it's merely a formality at this point."

Dorothy said feelingly, "I'm so sorry this happened, Nikki, dredging up painful memories for you."

"I know." Nikki agreed wholeheartedly, but was forever grateful she'd had their unwavering support throughout the ordeal. She was reluctant to tell them about the recent nightmare she had that forced her to relive the victimization in much too vivid detail for her comfort. But Gavin had brought her out of it and she hoped there would not be a repeat performance now that the threat Evigan presented seemed to be over. "Something positive has come out of it though," she indicated.

"Oh…?" Her mother favored her with a curious look.

Nikki told them about her protector during the crisis being none other than Brigette's former boyfriend, Gavin Lynley, now a special agent with the Mississippi Department of Corrections. They had been made aware of the acrimony at the time between Nikki and Gavin surrounding Brigette's death. Nikki would never have imagined that they would ever break the ice—and more…

"Really?" Dorothy touched her glasses. "Who would've thought?"

"How's that worked out?" William asked cautiously.

"You mentioned positive…?" her mother questioned.

"Yeah, we've made peace with the past," Nikki was happy to report, offering them a genuine smile. "Turns out that all we needed was a face-to-face to air out our grievances surrounding Brigette's death and find a way to work around them."

Dorothy smiled. "I'm so happy to hear that. You both lost someone you loved. Nothing can bring her back, but the fact that you and Gavin are on speaking terms now is a good thing in moving forward."

"I agree," her stepdad said.

"Thanks, guys," Nikki told them, and couldn't agree more herself. She thought about the kiss she and Gavin shared and couldn't help but wonder if there was more of their story to be told, in spite of the very real possibility that they were living together on borrowed time.

KNOWING THAT NIKKI was on the back deck speaking with her parents, Gavin thought it might be a good time to step out on the front porch and catch up with his ecologist sister, Lauren Nolden. Though they lived in different parts of the country and didn't get together as often as he would have liked, he still felt close to her and loved his nieces, Miley and Ellen, like they were his own children. He hoped one day to start a family, believing he had what it took to be a great father. The trick was bonding with a person who could be good marriage and mother material. He once thought that Brigette might fill those shoes, in spite of wondering if this was truly something she was made of. The fact that Nikki came to mind in that moment left Gavin wondering if it was possible that what he had been looking for had been staring him in the face all along, minus nearly a decade of time apart.

"What's up?" he said casually with a grin when his sister appeared on the screen of Gavin's cell phone for a video chat.

At thirty-three, Lauren was attractive with voluminous black hair in a Rezo cut and their mother's brown eyes. "I'm good," she said, smiling. "How about you?"

"Well," he began thoughtfully, "the man who murdered Brigette broke out of prison recently." Gavin recalled how Lauren had been there to help him pick up the pieces when he was still trying to make sense of it all.

"You're kidding?" Lauren's mouth hung wide in disbelief in what was obviously news to her. "How did I miss that?"

"With all the info on cable and social media on violent crime and violent criminals across the country these days, it wouldn't have been all that hard," he told her in all honesty. "But the good news is that it seems as though Perry Evigan is dead, having been located hiding at a farmhouse in Alabama, along with two other inmates who escaped."

"That is good to hear." Lauren's features softened.

"Having him on the loose, even for a day, must have had you climbing the walls," she voiced.

"Yeah, that about sums it up." Gavin furrowed his brow pensively. "There's more..."

"What?" his sister asked nervously.

He hesitated before replying, "I've gotten back in touch with Brigette's best friend, Nikki Sullivan." Gavin had shared his feelings at the time with Lauren on Nikki, in finding fault with her regarding Brigette's death. He knew now that this had been a big mistake and only wished he could take it back. But Nikki had forgiven him, more or less. Now he just needed to forgive himself.

"Oh, really?" Lauren gave him a long look. She had firmly rejected his position at the time, calling him misguided and unreasonable. "You're finally ready to bury the hatchet and acknowledge that Nikki was no more to blame as a crime victim than you were that Brigette fell prey to a callous serial killer?"

"Yeah, it's been buried," he told her happily. "Or at least we're getting there." Gavin glanced at the cottage, expecting Nikki to step outside. "I actually had my hand forced, so to speak, to make peace, in being assigned by the MDOC to protect Nikki while Evigan was still at large."

"I see." Lauren tilted her face to one side. "And now that the coast is clear...?"

He thought about the kiss they shared and general feeling of closeness developing between them. "We're going to keep in touch," he said sincerely, while thinking that could be an understatement when all was said and done.

"Good to hear. Something tells me that Brigette would believe it's the right way to go."

"I think so too." Even then, Gavin wondered if his former girlfriend would be on board as well were anything to develop with Nikki that moved more deeply into the romantic realm. Or would Brigette somehow view it as a betrayal from her boyfriend and best friend, even from beyond the grave? "Say hi to Miley and Ellen and Rory," Gavin said before disconnecting, only to find Nikki standing there. He wondered how much she had heard and what it might mean, if anything, moving forward.

NIKKI HAD OVERHEARD Gavin talking on the phone to his sister, Lauren. Though they had never met, Nikki sensed that they might have become friends had the opportunity presented itself back in the day—before disaster struck with Brigette's murder and Nikki's own brush with death. Along with Gavin's hostility toward her, lessening only slightly during her gut-wrenching testimony during Perry Evigan's trial, only to resume afterward. But things had taken a dramatic turn between her and Gavin since they got beyond their differences with his bodyguard duties. Didn't hurt matters any that they'd kissed. Or that he had been there when she'd had a recurrence of a nightmare involving Evigan trying to kill her.

Now, from what Nikki gathered, it appeared as though Lauren was in her corner—and had been all along—in believing that bygones should be bygones and Gavin and Nikki should have a camaraderie in modern times. At the very least.

"Hey," Nikki said evenly.

Gavin grinned easily at her. "Hey."

"Was that your sister?" she asked innocently.

"Yeah. Between work, marriage and two young kids, Lauren has her hands full these days."

"I'm sure." Nikki admired his sister for being able to juggle work and home life, as so many women did these days. She hoped to emulate this by becoming a wife and mother someday.

Gavin was thoughtful. "How are your parents doing?"

"Great! They're having the time of their lives in the Cayman Islands."

"How did they take the news about Perry Evigan?"

Nikki wrinkled her nose. "They were shocked to learn he had escaped from prison," she told him. "But were annoyed even more that I hadn't shared this with them sooner."

"Parents will be parents," he remarked understandably. "I'm sure they were relieved to know that the indications are that Evigan will no longer pose a threat to you or others."

"They were," Nikki conceded, just as his sister was. "Actually, on that note, I belong to a support group for survivors of disturbing events. We have a meeting this evening. In light of the recent events, I'd like to go as planned."

"Of course." Gavin stepped closer, meeting her eyes. "Mind if I tag along?" He paused. "Might do me some good to hear, outside of law enforcement, from others who have survived tragedies."

She nodded. "You're welcome to attend, Gavin." Nikki wondered if he might even wish to talk about what he went through with Brigette's murder, knowing that their perspectives were slightly different. Even if both arrived in the same place and suffered the same sense of loss.

He smiled. "Great. Hopefully, we'll both soon have closure with the official confirmation of Perry Evigan's death that you can share with the group at the next meeting as part of coming to terms with what happened to you."

"I hope so too." But for now, Nikki took solace in coming out on the other side of their shared experience and finding constructive ways of dealing with it.

Chapter Seven

Gavin was admittedly a little uneasy about attending the support group meeting, as he sat in the circle in the backyard surrounded by Japanese maple trees. Outside of family and a few friends, he had chosen to deal with his grief on his own. On the other hand, now seemed like a good time to, at the very least, show his support for Nikki as the group had obviously helped her deal with the victimization she'd gone through and also with what Brigette had experienced, paying the ultimate price by falling into the crosshairs of Perry Evigan.

After listening to Air Force vet Harry Rosen recount the horrors of war that resulted in the loss of a leg, Gavin watched as the host, Blair Roxburgh, went through her trauma, followed by a slender woman in her late twenties named Miriam Broderick. Running thin fingers nervously through her short, choppy brown hair with blond highlights, she blinked her green-brown eyes and recounted how her year older brother, Quint, had been the pedestrian victim of a hit-and-run driver a year ago. The driver had been under the influence of alcohol and antidepressants.

"Seeing Quint's life and bright future taken away in such a senseless fashion by an out-of-control driver who should never have been behind the wheel, shook up my whole world," Miriam expressed painfully. She wiped away tears and said, "Being in a support group like this has helped me to better process my loss and focus more on the good memories I have of my brother rather than the end of his journey."

Nikki, who sat next to her and sought to comfort her, then picked up where Miriam left off. She seemed to go back in time as Nikki's lower lip quivered when summarizing her ordeal at the hands of Perry Evigan, which included his brutal attack on Brigette.

While avoiding eye contact with Gavin in the chair next to her, Nikki uttered solemnly, "Honestly, I wasn't sure I'd ever make it out of Perry Evigan's house alive. Quite the opposite. When he murdered my best friend, I felt I was sure to follow." She sucked in a deep breath and now regarded Gavin feelingly. "But somehow, someway, I must have had an angel on my shoulder, as rescuers came before Evigan could make me another victim of a sexual assault and homicide by strangulation." Another deep sigh. "And here I am, able to tell my story. Including the fact that my attacker escaped from prison two days ago, before apparently meeting his fate in a fiery death. Karma can work for you and against you. This time, it seemed to have worked out right for society itself, by and large."

Though resisting any show of affection, Gavin was deeply moved by her heartfelt trip down memory lane, bringing him back to his own perspective of that fateful day a decade ago. He wished he had been there for Nikki when she needed him most as someone who could relate to what she was going through. Now, as fortune would have it, he was given a second chance to make up for lost time, if she let him.

Blair, who sat across the circle, leaned back in her chair and said, "Gavin, why don't you tell us a little about yourself—and anything else you feel comfortable sharing regarding what you've gone through…"

Feeling put on the spot, Gavin felt ready nonetheless to get off his chest something he probably should have a long time ago. He eyed Nikki, whose expression was one of encouragement, and said equably, "My name's Gavin Lynley. I currently work as a special agent for the Mississippi Department of Corrections, Special Operations Unit. And, no," he joked to lighten the mood, "I'm not here to haul anyone off to jail." He got a chuckle or two in response, including one from Nikki. "Ten years ago, I was still a correctional employee, but also the boyfriend of someone who was a victim of a sexual assault before being murdered." He choked back the words, as the image of her final moments was hard to digest. "I was supposed to hang out with Brigette that night, but had to go into work at the last moment and, as such, was forced to cancel the date…"

Gavin paused and felt the empathetic hand of Nikki's on his. "Needless to say, it's haunted me ever since, to one degree or another, knowing that if I had only made different choices back then, Brigette would almost certainly be alive today—" He favored Nikki with an emotional gaze and said, squeezing her hand, "But through some means, Brigette's best friend—Nikki—was able to survive being a victim of the same psychopath and serial killer." He took a breath, looked away and then back at her. "I admit that there was a time when I tried to blame Nikki for something that obviously wasn't her fault. I deeply regret that now. The fault for what happened to her and Brigette lies entirely with the man who drugged and attacked them. I can't express enough how glad I am that Nikki didn't suffer the same fate as Brigette—and has found a way to get past that time in her life and make something out of it."

"Thank you for saying that," she whispered to him, her eyes watering.

"It's been long overdue," he returned with sincerity.

Blair smiled at him and said, "Owning up to past mistakes, while sharing your own story of loss, regrets and moving forward, is commendable, Gavin."

He grinned sideways. "It's a step or two in the right direction anyway," he allowed, knowing it would take more to make things right with Nikki—and himself, for that matter.

The host then invited another survivor to speak as Gavin listened, while focusing largely on Nikki and wanting to see her gain greater closure once they knew that Perry Evigan was indeed dead and soon to be buried.

AFTER THE SESSION was over, Blair pulled Nikki to the side and said, "It was good of you to bring Gavin along, seeing that you two have so much in common with the ordeal you both went through."

"I'm glad he came too," Nikki admitted, not at all sure that would happen. She supposed he needed to let out what was bottled up in him all these years to a wider audience.

"Having your tormentor escape and then be stopped in his tracks must have sent you on a roller coaster of emotions."

"Yes." Nikki made a face. "I'm afraid my stomach is still tied up in knots as I process everything."

"I'm sure." Blair put a hand on her arm. "Staying in

touch with Gavin should do wonders to get you over the hump."

Nikki glanced at Gavin, who was chatting with Harry Rosen. "That's the plan," she told her. Even if she was unsure to what extent. "Hope you can make it to my art exhibit tomorrow?"

Blair flashed her teeth. "You couldn't keep me away if you tried."

Nikki laughed, happy to have her busy friend in attendance. "I was hoping you'd say that."

They joined others and made small talk, before Gavin asked Nikki, holding her elbow, "Are you ready to head out?"

She felt his touch and warmed to a grin playing askew on his lips, responding accordingly, "Yes, I think so."

The drive back to the cottage was mostly quiet. Nikki was sure that Gavin was getting back in touch with his feelings for Brigette, now that he had bared his soul in talking about the crime and losing his girlfriend. For her part, Nikki felt grateful that Gavin had gotten past accusing her of not doing enough to keep Brigette from going out that fateful night, as he seemed to acknowledge that Brigette was old enough to make her own choices in deciding what she wanted to do in her life from one day to the next.

The same had been true for Nikki. She had been restless that Saturday night and relished the opportunity to have some fun with her best friend. Especially when not that far removed from having ended things with her disastrous boyfriend at the time, Felix Kovell. How could she or Brigette have known that they were headed into a hornet's nest when they went to Johnnie's Shack nightclub, where Perry Evigan lay in wait like the evil vulture he was, lulling them into a false sense of security?

Obviously, she should have relied on her instincts that told Nikki that Evigan was very bad news and they should never have invited him back to their table for another round of drinks. But she rejected this in favor of trying to make her best friend happy—at least for the moment—in the absence of Gavin, whom Brigette didn't seem the least bit put off about that he'd left her hanging.

I can't change history, Nikki told herself candidly. She glanced over at Gavin behind the wheel and wondered if it was possible to change the future. Or their future, by taking a step back to the past. Or would they do more harm than good were she to spill the beans about Brigette to the man who clearly had never gotten over her? Spoiling his fantasy, perhaps, about the one whom he missed his chance with by virtue of a serial killer.

After having a nightcap, during which they spoke mainly about the near certainty of Perry Evigan's timely demise and the weight that would be lifted off their collective shoulders, Nikki and Gavin went to their separate rooms with just a simple good-night.

To Nikki, this was the best way to go. Even if she was undeniably interested in Gavin—whether it was wise or not—a one-night stand with someone soon on his way out the door was simply not in the cards. She doubted it was something he wanted either. And since a steady relationship seemed unlikely, why do anything they both would likely regret?

That night, Nikki tossed and turned in bed. Only this time, she wasn't having a nightmare about Perry Evigan, the Gulfport Nightmare Killer. Instead, she found herself dreaming about Brigette and the different faces of guys other than Gavin that she was cozying up to. Seemed as though her best friend had made a habit of two-timing Gavin right under his nose. That was so not cool, Nikki knew. But it wasn't her place to expose Brigette then.

And what about now?

That last thought was enough to wake Nikki from the deep sleep and disturbing dream. Though she felt her heart racing and was perspiring, she must not have made any sounds that resonated, as Gavin never showed up in her room to snap her out of it. She was glad, as Nikki wasn't sure how she would have responded had he asked about the dream. How might she have come across to him, in tarnishing what was obviously someone he had placed on a pedestal?

Climbing out of bed, Nikki went downstairs barefoot for a glass of water. Part of her wished Gavin would come down too, if only to talk. But he never did. She drank the water and went back to bed. It took a while, but she finally fell back to sleep. In the process, she'd debated whether or not to be honest with Gavin, as she would have wanted him to do with her had the shoe been on the other foot, before an answer came as clear as day.

WHEN GAVIN CAME down in the morning, he saw that Nikki had made breakfast. He noted that her hair was in a high ponytail and she had on jogging clothes and running shoes. Unlike last night, when she was probably wearing something similar to the red chemise lingerie nightgown she'd had on the previous night, conjuring up intimate images in his head. He'd heard her come downstairs and actually considered joining her for perhaps a nightcap, but decided against it. He'd invaded her space enough by his very presence, which, for better or worse, was close to running its course.

"Hey." He gave her a grin.

"Good morning." She returned the smile. "Hope you're in the mood for blueberry waffles with orange juice and coffee?"

"Sounds great," he said, stepping closer in his bare feet, while wearing tapered jeans and a casual shirt. "Can I help?"

"Feel free to take your plate to the table," she said, handing it to him with the steaming waffle.

Gavin did just that as he studied her. Seemed like there was something on her mind. He'd picked up on this ever since the support group gathering. Or, more specifically, ever since he had chosen to speak about his own ordeal ten years ago. So what was it? Had the trip down memory lane, mixed with the fall of their nemesis, Perry Evigan, messed with her head? Or was bringing Brigette back to the forefront a bad idea?

He waited till they were both seated across the black-and-pecan wooden corner breakfast nook table, before Gavin asked Nikki straightforwardly over his coffee mug, "Is there something you want to talk about…?"

She sliced the knife perfectly into her waffle, stuck the fork in and held it there, and gazed at him for a long moment, then said tentatively, "I've been debating whether or not to say anything…"

He cocked his brow curiously. "Regarding?"

"Brigette." Nikki set her fork down and tasted the orange juice.

"What about Brigette?" Gavin asked, but had a feeling he knew where this was going.

Hesitating again, Nikki responded, "First, let me just say I loved her like the sister I never had, in spite of our differences in personalities and styles…" She swallowed thickly and looked him in the eye. "I know you loved Brigette too, which makes this all the harder to say."

"Just get it out, Nikki," he pressed, resting his arms on the table in wait.

"All right." She sighed. "I hate to speak ill of the dead, especially after your impassioned thoughts about Brigette and how her life ended. But now that we've gotten to know each other better—along with the fact that I might not get another chance to be perfectly honest with you once you leave Owl's Bay—I think it's only fair you know that Brigette was not the loyal girlfriend you may have believed she was in plotting a future with her at the time…"

Gavin knitted his brows and raised a hand to stop Nikki from going further. "I know that," he said flatly.

Her eyes widened. "You do?"

"Yeah, of course." Whether he wanted to face up to the truth or not, Gavin knew it was high time he did just that. Especially if he had any hope at all of beginning something with Nikki without the specter of Brigette coming between them. Holding Nikki's intent gaze, he continued thoughtfully, "I caught her once making out with another guy. I knew then that she'd likely gone even further with him or others. On some level, I think I always knew she wasn't faithful to the relationship or took it as seriously as I did—but I chose to ignore this, believing I had what it took to make her see things my way." Gavin sat back, ruminating. "Guess it was just an ego thing. No one ever wants to accept defeat in a romance, no matter how challenging. When Brigette was murdered, I was at the point of ending things with her, realizing that we just weren't right for each other. But I never got that chance. Feeling guilty that I hadn't been there for her at the end, I chose instead to blame you for what happened. Along the way, I managed to push out of my mind the reality that Brigette and I were through, for all intents and purposes. Perry Evigan—that bastard—deprived me of the opportunity to ever tell Brigette."

"I'm sorry," Nikki expressed sincerely. "Sorry I ever brought this up."

"Don't be," he argued in earnest, forking a slice of waffle and coating it with maple syrup off the plate. "It needed to be said. If you hadn't done so, I would have, sooner rather than later. We both cared for Brigette and that can never die. But we also owe it to ourselves to put those feelings and the times that they represented to rest properly—especially since it appears that Evigan is no longer around to keep the dark memories alive and poisoning the atmosphere."

"You're right. It still feels a little weird though."

"For me too." He met her eyes musingly. "But it feels more right to get it out in the open and recalibrate our lives beyond Brigette—wherever that takes us—accordingly."

Nikki showed her teeth, indicating they were on the same page in that respect. "Okay."

He smiled back, feeling as though they had turned a corner, no matter what might be around it. "Good."

They finished eating and then she told him nonchalantly, "I'm going out for a run."

"I'll go with you," he said, knowing that until it became official that Evigan was no longer a threat, Gavin wasn't about to take any chances in making her a target of the serial killer.

"Think you can keep up?" Nikki challenged him.

"I can try." He expected he would do more than that, in spite of jogging not being his forte, per se, as an exercise option. "Let me get into my running shoes."

NIKKI FELT A huge sigh of relief that Gavin hadn't thought she was overstepping by spilling the beans about Brigette. Not only did he believe it was the right thing to do, but he'd also already known that Brigette was not as into the relationship as he was. Gavin had planned to break up with her, but had been deprived of this by Perry Evigan.

So where does that leave us? Nikki asked herself bewilderingly as she ran in front of Gavin down the tree-lined sidewalk, with him keeping pace like running was as natural for him as it was for her. She wouldn't deny having feelings for the good-looking special agent. She sensed it was more than a one-way street. Might they be able to turn it into a real romance, now that everything was out in the open? Or would their shared past continue to stand in the way of any type of future—with Evigan seemingly now out of the picture and Gavin no longer having a legitimate excuse for remaining in town much longer?

"Remind me why I agreed to this?" he quipped, catching up to her and breaking the reverie.

"Because you're in great shape and working those long legs comes with the territory in your business. Piece of cake," Nikki added with a smile.

Gavin breathed out of his nose. "Then it's a good thing

I have a sweet tooth for tasty desserts, including caramel cake and lemon cake—or need I remind you of that?"

"How can I forget?" She faced him while recalling how he went to town on her leftover apple pie. "As for those cakes, I'll have to look into that." Nikki wondered if he planned to stick around long enough to give her a reason to accept his kitchen challenge.

"Fair enough." He brushed shoulders and asked, "Is that a hill I see up ahead?"

"Afraid so." She chuckled as they approached it. "Is that going to be a problem?"

"I think I can manage," Gavin told her with a laugh. "I'll wait for you up there." He suddenly took off, leaving her in the dust.

It took Nikki only a moment to recover before she went after him, while feeling she could get used to these mini challenges. And more, should it come to that.

When she got to the top of the hill, Nikki saw that Gavin was on his cell phone. From the gist of it, she gathered that he was talking to his boss. Between Gavin's disturbed expression and switching the phone to his other ear, she knew it was not good news.

But just how bad it truly was registered when Nikki heard him voice sourly, "You mean Perry Evigan is still alive—?"

Chapter Eight

"It sure as hell looks that way," Director Whitfield stated on the cell phone, as Gavin listened while eyeing Nikki, who had clearly picked up on the conversation once she caught up to him on the hill.

As it was, Gavin saw no benefit in keeping the disturbing news from Nikki that Perry Evigan was not in the farmhouse when it caught on fire, leaving three bodies charred. But he could at least delay this till they got back to her cottage. He asked Whitfield to hold that thought.

After surveying the area and seeing no signs of trouble, Gavin led the way in a quick and steady dash down the hill, while both he and Nikki stayed close to each other, a tense silence between them. For his part, Gavin was still caught up in seeing Brigette's betrayal in a new light, his growing feelings toward Nikki and how Perry Evigan's being seemingly still on the loose might impact their ability to move forward.

At the cottage, Gavin got Whitfield back on the phone, letting his boss know he was on speaker, and after meeting Nikki's keen gaze he said to the director in a straightforward tone of voice, "You were saying about Evigan and the farmhouse fire—"

"As you know, we pulled out three bodies—or what

was left of them—from the burned-out location," Whitfield said intently. "Working with the St. Clair County Medical Examiner and Coroner's Office, a forensic dentist, Dr. Allie Tagomori, compared the dental records of the three escapees to the teeth belonging to the charred corpses. Well, two of the victims were officially identified as Aaron Machado and Craig Schneider. The third victim's teeth were not a match for Perry Evigan's dental records," the director lamented.

"How is that even possible?" Gavin furrowed his forehead, but he knew the answer, in spite of the improbability of the decedent being someone other than Evigan.

Whitfield responded knowingly, "Well, it looks like Perry Evigan was never even at the farmhouse, as shocking and disappointing as that is. He must have decided at some point to separate himself from the other escaped cons. Turns out to have been a good move on his part," the director admitted. "As arson investigators sifted through the charred wreckage, indications are that the fire was set deliberately by someone inside the farmhouse. Apparently, one or all of the fugitives had no intention of going back to prison alive."

The fiery ending at the farmhouse notwithstanding, to Gavin, it was less about Evigan making a good move or being smarter, per se, than the other fugitives from justice, and more a matter of being much luckier than them when he needed this most.

"So, who was the other victim of the fire?" Gavin asked, gazing at Nikki, who was undoubtedly just as curious as him.

"Turns out, it was an ex-con named Merrill Carlyle," Whitfield said. "Dr. Tagomori was able to create a DNA profile from the decedent's teeth that was entered into CODIS and came back with a hit on Carlyle. He was the cellmate of Aaron Machado. Carlyle was serving time for armed robbery before being released four months ago. Apparently, he and Machado kept in touch and rendezvoused at some point during the escapees' journey, and Carlyle chose to stay with them."

Gavin set his jaw, again turning to Nikki and her stunned reaction. "Any clue on the whereabouts of Perry Evigan?"

Whitfield made a sighing sound, then replied without elaboration, "We have reason to believe that Evigan may be attempting to evade capture by heading to Mexico. Information was found in his cell about Guadalajara. He could be driving a white Chevrolet Malibu. Someone matching Evigan's description was reported stealing such a vehicle from a shopping center parking lot in Blytheville, Arkansas. We're looking into it."

"With all due respect, that's not very reassuring as to Evigan's whereabouts," Gavin offered candidly, believing there was still a good chance that the escaped serial killer had no intention of leaving the country. "I'm still worried that Evigan may try to come after Nikki Sullivan." Gavin met her unreadable eyes. "For that reason—" and others he chose to keep to himself, such as wanting to remain in Nikki's company while they sorted out their feelings for one another "—if it's all the same to you, Director Whitfield, I'd rather stay with her as long as Evigan remains on the loose." *And who knows how long that could be?* Gavin told himself, seeing how resourceful the fugitive had proven to be at eluding capture, thus far.

Without prelude, Whitfield was in agreement. "Yeah,

that's probably a good idea. You can stay with Ms. Sullivan for now." The director waited a beat, then warned, "Just don't get too comfortable with this arrangement, Lynley. You do have other assignments," Gavin was reminded. "Wherever he's holed up, Perry Evigan has probably heard by now about his fellow escapees' fiery demise. Not to mention having every law enforcement officer in the country on the lookout for him. As such, he's likely not to want to go anywhere near her while on the lam with the authorities in hot pursuit. If it becomes necessary, we'll see to it that Ms. Sullivan has a personal protection detail to keep her safe."

"That's good enough for me," Gavin told him, sure that he was skating on thin ice in wanting to continue as Nikki's primary bodyguard while Evigan remained at large. But he would take whatever the director was giving him in allowing Gavin to use their time together to protect her and bond with her further.

"ARE YOU KIDDING ME?" Nikki's eyes narrowed at Gavin as they stood in the living room, where he had just ended his phone conversation with Marvin Whitfield. "I can't believe that Perry Evigan has managed to remain free while the two other convicts he escaped from prison with are dead—"

"I know." Gavin turned to her sympathetically. "It's just one of those things. He played his cards right this time. The next time, he might not be so lucky."

"And I'm supposed to put my life on hold till Evigan runs out of luck?" she complained, arms crossed petulantly, even as Nikki knew that the chances the serial killer would actually get his bloody hands on her again were nil at best. Particularly when Gavin had talked his boss into allowing him to stick around as her armed, much of the time, protector. She certainly wasn't complaining. Quite the opposite, in fact. Having him around for a while longer was just what Nikki needed to see what flames might erupt from the smoke that seemed to be swirling around them at every turn and was given room to grow now that the air had been cleared regarding Brigette.

In her reverie, Nikki barely realized that Gavin had drawn her very near to his body as he said attentively, "You should definitely keep your life going as normal as possible, with only some minor adjustments temporarily. Such as sharing your lovely cottage with me. And, of course, being aware of your surroundings and who might be lurking about. Or not." She felt his warm breath on her cheek as Gavin added, "Of course, I'll be around to make sure Perry Evigan doesn't get any wild ideas and try to act upon them in targeting you again for his sick impulses."

"That's nice to know," she had to admit, even if just how long it would last was unsettling, to say the least. She regarded him. "So, do you really think Evigan could show up here, even with all the heat he's facing, constantly needing to look over both shoulders and then some?"

"You never know," Gavin said with a straight face, still with his hands at her waist. "I gave up trying to figure out serial killers with a pathologically warped mind a long time ago. What I can tell you though, is that I don't want you to spend too much time worrying about the likes of Perry Evigan. Though he's still on the loose, the man is basically yesterday's news where we're concerned."

Nikki wasn't sure he truly believed that, considering Gavin's very—and strong—presence in her life. But she was happy to go along with it on both fronts. "In that case," she told him casually, "I suppose I can feel free to stick with the exhibition I have for this evening at an art gallery downtown?"

"Absolutely!" Gavin said smoothly. "No reason to cancel what you've been planning in showcasing your amazing talents," he insisted. "I'd love to see your art on display—and maybe I'll even buy a piece to put on the wall in my great room that's pretty barren."

"Hmm..." She smiled, trying to imagine the layout of his house. Would he ever invite her there, once his time in Owl's Bay was up? "In that case, I'd better head to my studio to put the finishing touches on one more painting to be in the exhibit."

"All right. And one more thing..." He cast his eyes upon hers, tilted his face, and Gavin moved slowly toward her lips as though to give Nikki an out in case he was overstepping his bounds. But she had no desire to do such a thing, and raised her chin just enough to accept the kiss.

Shutting her eyes, Nikki took in his hard mouth, opening her own slightly to perfectly contour with his, as she clung to him like he was all hers—at least while they kissed. But as her senses came back and Nikki realized she needed to restrain her desire for the man, she pulled their lips apart and, meeting his gaze, asked, "Is this another caught-up-in-the-moment show of weakness...?"

He held her stare and, tasting his lips, said frankly, "I think we both know it goes beyond that."

"Just checking." She grinned at him while acknowledging, "I think so too. But I still needed to hear you say it."

"I'm saying it," he affirmed solidly.

"Good." Nikki left it there, knowing she still had some

work to do before the showing. And she also wanted to give them time to assess where this could lead and just how far and wide, once a serial killer was truly left in the rearview mirror once and for all.

ON A DIRT ROAD, Perry Evigan was driving a stolen gray Buick Encore, having ditched the Chevrolet Malibu he had stolen earlier in Blytheville, Arkansas, after making his way back to Mississippi. With unfinished business, a decade in the making, he was on a mission and would not be denied.

He considered the unfortunate deaths of his fellow escapees, Craig Schneider and Aaron Machado, along with Aaron's former cellmate, Merrill Carlyle. Perry couldn't honestly say that he was surprised. He knew that the authorities were gunning for them. He also knew that none of the fugitives—himself included—had any intention of going back to prison. Which was precisely why he separated himself from the others, as Perry believed his will to survive was far stronger than theirs.

As was his determination to get the one who managed to survive the power of his hands meant to strangle her to death. Just like her friend, Brigette. And his other conquests.

Nikki Sullivan.

Perry thought back to when he first spotted the news about the object of his desire to kill while accessing the prison's library services. The piece was entitled, "Prominent Local Artist to Showcase Work at Owl's Bay Art Gallery."

That artist was none other than Nikki Sullivan, the near victim he could never quite get out of his system. Now he was free and had another chance to go after her, to do with as he pleased. Before strangling her to death like the others. The mere thought excited him no end.

The exhibition was tonight in Owl's Bay.

If lucky, maybe he could make it on time to rain down on her parade.

Perry laughed at the thought, but then turned dead serious, knowing that it was anything but a laughing matter. At least not until the deed was done.

WHILE NIKKI WAS upstairs getting ready for her big art exhibit, Gavin took a video call from his cousin, Russell Lynley. He watched as Russell's square face appeared on the cell phone screen. Gray-eyed and black-haired, in a high, tight cut style, they were the same age. Like Russell's brother, Scott, he was an FBI special agent, working out of the field office in Houston, Texas, while specializing in serial killer and domestic terrorist cases.

"Hey," Gavin said evenly.

"Hey." Russell gave a little grin before turning serious. "Heard that Perry Evigan has somehow managed to dodge the fate of his fellow escapees."

"Yeah, looks that way." Gavin leaned back as he sat on a wicker accent armchair in the living room. "The man seems to have nine lives—as if to add up to the number of women he murdered plus one."

"He only has one life," Russell said firmly. "And its shelf life is hardly inexhaustible. FBI agents are working overtime with your guys to nab him, or otherwise stop him in his tracks."

"I know and I'm sure it's only a matter of time before we get him. But it's the wait that's driving me crazy—

not knowing where he is at the moment and what he's up to..." Gavin drew a breath as he pictured the creep killing Brigette and damned near ending Nikki's life as well.

"I hear you," Russell put forth, his thick brows knitting. "I know you're concerned that Evigan might try to come after the surviving witness, Nikki Sullivan—"

"The thought has crossed my mind," he responded wryly. "Which is why I'm doing guard duty as long as Evigan stays a fugitive." Gavin knew that his interest in Nikki had moved well beyond a professional obligation, but there was no reason to go there just yet. So long as the threat remained for her safety, first and foremost.

"It won't be long." Russell narrowed his eyes thoughtfully. "Have you two been able to reconcile with everything that went down with Brigette?"

"Yeah." Gavin nodded. "Nikki was every bit as much a victim of Evigan as Brigette," he acknowledged. "I get that now and only want to make sure she gets to live the life she's entitled to and that was taken away from Brigette."

"She will," Russell sought to reassure him, before they spoke briefly about a case he was working on as part of a task force that included Russell's wife, Rosamund, a Homeland Security Investigations special agent.

When Gavin got off the line, he spotted Nikki coming down the stairs. Taking one look at her in a figure-flattering, floral surplice jersey dress, worn with strappy black sandals and her long hair in a plaited bun, made his jaw drop. "Wow! You look amazing," he told her, getting to his feet.

Nikki blushed. "Why, thank you." She eyed him. "You're not so bad yourself, mister."

He grinned at the compliment but downplayed it nonetheless. "Guess it was a smart idea to bring along a set of nicer clothing," he said, wearing a crisp lilac dress shirt, navy slacks and black loafers. "Anyway, this evening is all about you, Nikki. I'm only along for the ride." *And to keep my eyes open for any signs of Perry Evigan*, Gavin told himself.

"I'm glad you could come," she told him, meeting his steady gaze. "That's good enough for me."

"Same here."

Both ignored mentioning the part where an escaped serial killer threatened to cast a dark shadow over the art exhibition.

Chapter Nine

At the Owl's Bay Art Gallery on Fellows Street, Nikki was ecstatic over having her art works on display. Though this wasn't her first merry-go-round, she did feel a little extra burst of adrenaline in having Gavin there to see what she brought to the table. It was also comforting to know that the special agent for the Mississippi Department of Corrections had her back, just in case Perry Evigan did decide to make an appearance.

Even if a part of her felt this was unlikely, given that the search was on to recapture the escaped con, Nikki wasn't about to let her guard down as long as he was still out there somewhere. *I can't let him get to me*, she told herself with determination, while surveying her portrait, landscape and still-life oil paintings with Gavin.

"So, what do you think?" she asked, gazing up at him as they both held flutes of champagne.

"I think you're incredible," he told her. His eyes lit up as he peered at a landscape work of art and then shifted his focus to look at a painting of a bowl of red and green apples.

Nikki laughed. "I bet you say that to all the girls." One she knew for a fact he did once upon a time.

Gavin chuckled. "Trust me, I don't. I know talent when

I see it—and so much more." He met her gaze and she could tell that the compliment went beyond her artistic skills.

"That's nice to know." She flushed and tasted the champagne. "Hopefully, there will still come a time when I can paint you," she threw out, already imagining the thrill of getting him on canvas.

"Count on it," he said confidently as Gavin sipped his own champagne.

They moved on and were joined by Blair Roxburgh and her boyfriend, Oliver Pascal, a tall, fifty-something chiropractor with shoulder-length, swept-back salt-and-pepper hair and a matching egg-shaped full beard. He touched his octagon glasses while turning blue eyes on Nikki, and said, "Your paintings are stunning."

"I told you they were out of this world," Blair marveled, holding a flute of champagne.

"We're all in agreement there," Gavin pitched in.

"Thank you all," Nikki said, grinning from ear to ear. Getting praise from people she knew gave Nikki all the validation she needed that this was what she was meant to do with her life. She told them humbly, "I'm still forever a work in progress as an artist, but I'm honing my craft with each painting."

"That you are, indeed." Blair smiled at her and raised her flute glass in toast, with everyone joining in.

"So this is where you've been hiding in plain view…"

Nikki heard the lyrical voice and turned to see the gallery owner, Jillian Yamaguchi. In her late sixties and a great artist in her own right, she was frail and had fine white hair in a chignon bun. "You found me," Nikki joked, and introduced her to everyone.

"Good." Jillian's brown eyes crinkled. She cupped an arm beneath Nikki's and said, "Hope you don't mind if I steal her away for a bit? I have some people I want to introduce Nikki to, while playing up her exhibition."

Nikki looked to Gavin, in particular, for his approval and he nodded. "Please, go mingle with your audience. I'll try to stay out of your way."

She knew that meant he wouldn't go too far, in case she needed him. "Okay."

"We'll just check out more of your works," Blair told her, holding hands with Oliver.

"I'll find you later," Nikki told them, and headed off with Jillian.

GAVIN WATCHED NIKKI walk away with the gallery owner before he began wandering around, looking this way and that for any indication that Perry Evigan had made his way to the art gallery. Admittedly, it seemed like a giant leap to believe that the fugitive serial killer would actually have the wherewithal to track Nikki down in this location, at this time. But Gavin had been in law enforcement and corrections long enough to know that hardened and tenacious criminals could never be underestimated. That was certainly true for Evigan, who had managed to strangle to death ten women without being caught, before he finally had the hammer dropped on him.

The man had walked away from a maximum-security prison farm and remained on the loose for days, while his fellow escapees had perished in a fire. That alone told Gavin that Evigan was not one to be taken lightly, no matter the odds against his taking another shot at Nikki.

As a result, Gavin found himself checking out anyone and everyone who was anywhere near Nikki, while maintaining a good enough distance to allow her to bask in her success as a local artist. *I don't want to see Evigan spoil her showing by trying to take Nikki out*, Gavin told himself. She'd paid a high enough price for her earlier victimization by him. Not to mention, witnessing the sexual assault and murder of her best friend. Gavin would not allow Nikki to go through that again—so long as he was able to stick around and protect her while her attacker was out there.

He moved beyond the perimeter to see if anyone else matching the serial killer's general description came into view. Nothing. Breathing a sigh of relief, Gavin continued to walk around and took out his cell phone. He called Special Agent Jean O'Reilly. She picked up immediately.

"Hey," he told her. "Any news on Perry Evigan and his whereabouts…?"

"The assumption is still that he's headed for Mexico," she reported. "But I'm not so sure about that. Evigan, who thinks he's smarter than everyone else—and seemed to spend much of his time in prison educating himself even more—doesn't strike me as someone who would be happy spending the rest of his life south of the border."

Gavin had the same thought, but asked, "What about the material on Guadalajara found in Evigan's cell?"

"From what I understand, it belonged to his cellmate, José Contreras, another convicted murderer, who came to this country as an illegal immigrant sex trafficker, by way of Guadalajara."

"Hmm…" Gavin muttered. "So, Evigan could pretty much be headed or hiding anywhere." *Even in Owl's Bay*, Gavin thought, but tried to push that notion away.

"True," Jean said, "but it appears that he might be moving toward the Midwest, or farther away from Mississippi. The white Chevrolet Malibu Evigan was believed to have been driving was found abandoned in Arkansas. Someone matching his description was reportedly spotted in Indiana."

Maybe he isn't anywhere near Owl's Bay, Gavin thought, glancing about at the art lovers who showed up. Could be that he was giving Evigan far more credit than he deserved. Or maybe there was good reason to feel uneasy for as long as the escaped killer was not back behind bars.

"Keep me in the loop for anything else you find out," Gavin told her, knowing that he was just a bit preoccupied to be in the midst of the hunt for the Gulfport Nightmare Killer.

"You've got it," Jean promised, and Gavin hung up, realizing he'd managed to lose sight of Nikki and needed to find her in a hurry, to make sure she was all right.

"This is Kenan Fernández." Jillian introduced the man she had described as an art lover.

Nikki cocked a brow with dismay as she stared at the personal trainer she thought she had seen the last of. "Kenan…" she gasped.

Jillian looked from one to the other. "Do you two know each other…?"

"We've crossed paths," Kenan responded, a smug grin on his lips.

"Something like that." Nikki peered at him, then told Jillian, "Can you give us a moment…?"

"Of course." Jillian flashed her a mildly concerned look. "Find me when you're through."

"I will." Nikki offered her a gentle smile and watched Jillian walk away; then Nikki scanned the room for Gavin, who seemed to have disappeared. But something told her that it wouldn't be for long. She glared at Kenan and snapped, "You shouldn't be here."

His brows joined. "Why shouldn't I? You invited me to your showing, don't you remember?"

Nikki had forgotten this and wished she could take it back. "That was before I realized that we weren't right for each other," she told him candidly. "You know it, I know it." She had blocked him on her cell phone. "Now I'd like you to leave, Kenan."

He scowled at her. "You can't get rid of me that easily," he spat. "I think there's still something between us. If you'd only get off your high horse and let it happen."

She shot him an icy stare. "Are we really going to do this—here? I have an art exhibition underway with lots of people around. Be smart, Kenan. Stalking is a crime, whether you want to believe it or not."

"Believe it!" Gavin's voice boomed as he came up from behind her. He got in Kenan's face and said, "I thought we understood each other?"

Kenan held his ground as best he could. "You thought wrong."

Gavin pulled out and flashed his identification. "I'm a special agent with the Mississippi Department of Corrections. One phone call and I'll have you arrested and charged with aggravated stalking," he asserted. "If convicted, you could serve five years in prison. Believe me, you don't want to end up there." Gavin allowed that to sink in and asked toughly, "So, what's it going to be? Will you leave Nikki alone?"

Kenan set his jaw. He eyed Nikki like a man who seemed still obsessed with her, but appeared to know when he was outnumbered and backed into a corner. Throwing his hands up, he muttered, "Yeah, whatever."

Nikki watched him storm off and said under her breath, "Hope he's finally gotten the message this time."

"So do I." Gavin frowned. "But in case he's still bent on harassing you, I think you need to take out a protective order against the man. If Fernández tries to circumvent it, he'll get himself further into hot water that won't end well for him."

"I'll do it," Nikki was quick to agree. "I've about had it up to here—" she raised her hand to her chin "—with him. If it takes a restraining order for him to back off, so be it." *And having you around as my bodyguard is certainly an extra deterrent*, Nikki told herself thankfully.

"Good." Gavin smiled at her warmly. "Anything else interesting happen since I left…?"

"Only that everyone seems to love my artwork," she answered, but sensed that he was referring to any sign that Perry Evigan had decided to pay her an unwelcome visit too. "No sighting of Evigan, thus far, knock on wood."

"I doubt that he'll show his face around here," Gavin spoke confidently. "He's got too much to lose by coming after the one living—and protected—witness to his serial crimes. Besides, Evigan's allegedly been seen in Indiana in his quest to evade recapture."

Though feeling relieved to hear this, Nikki still had to ask, "Do you think that's true?"

He hesitated before responding. "Perhaps. But we won't really know till Evigan's back in custody and we can interrogate him and see exactly what path he took to avoid capture."

"Well, that time can't come soon enough," she declared anxiously.

Gavin nodded. "I'm with you there."

"How's everything going?" Jillian asked when joining them.

"We're good," Nikki told her, glancing at Gavin.

"Yeah, she's all yours." He grinned as he looked at the art gallery owner.

Jillian smiled. "Actually, this evening, Nikki is not just mine, but everyone's artist extraordinaire."

"I couldn't agree more." Gavin flashed Nikki a devastating smile and she took it in, while masking her growing desire to be with him in ways that had nothing to do with his safeguarding role in her life.

WHEN THEY GOT back to the cottage, Gavin double-checked the perimeter for his own peace of mind that there was no indication it had been broken into, that they had been followed, or otherwise suggested that Perry Evigan had been there. Or even Kenan Fernández, for that matter. Though both men had more reasons for staying away than coming there, at risk to their freedom, Gavin wasn't convinced that common sense and logic would overcome obsession, irrationality and stupidity, where it concerned the two men.

I have no problem going the extra mile to protect Nikki from any potential predators, Gavin thought, knowing full well that this had become personal, as much as his duty for the MDOC. He needed Nikki to stay alive and well, so they had the opportunity to take what had been given them in each other and run with it.

They entered the house and Nikki punched in the code to the security system, after which Gavin took a quick walk-through with Nikki close by, before he told her levelly when they were back downstairs, "Looks like the coast is clear."

"That's nice to know," she said. "I would hate to think of this cottage as ground zero for a serial killer on the prowl. But thanks for checking."

"Not a problem." *Not yet anyway*, he thought, and wanted to keep it that way. Gavin turned his attention away from threats to her big art exhibit. "It was fun seeing you in your element this evening. Your paintings, on full display, were incredible. And so are you."

Nikki blushed. "I try my best. Sometimes even that falls short, but what can you say?"

He grinned. "Not everything needs to be said. There are things that speak for themselves."

"You're quite the philosopher," she said with an amused chuckle. "So, I guess I'll allow my artwork to do the talking for me—and add my two cents every now and then."

Gavin laughed. "Seems like a pretty good plan of action."

She smiled and headed into the kitchen. "Would you like a glass of wine?"

"Sure, that sounds good."

He followed her and watched as she took the bottle of white wine from the stainless-steel fridge and removed two wineglasses from a cabinet. After filling each halfway, she handed him a glass and, after sipping from her own, said, "It's been nice having you here and getting reacquainted."

"I feel the same way," he made clear, putting the glass

to his lips. "I wish it had been sooner to reach this point in time, but getting to know you now has been well worth the wait."

"I agree wholeheartedly." She beamed. "That is, getting to know the man you are today."

Gavin stared into her entrancing blue eyes and knew instinctively that this was the right moment to kiss her again. He cupped her chin and went for it, pressing their lips together for a stirring kiss that upped his desire for her a few notches.

As though she were reading his mind and matching it with her own, Nikki met his eyes and cooed sotto voce, "I want to get you into bed."

His libido soared even more. "I'd like nothing more than to make love to you, Nikki," he told her with a sense of urgency.

"Then what are you waiting for?" she challenged him. "Make love to me—now…"

In his head, Gavin imagined ripping her clothes off, lifting her onto the countertop and engaging in primordial sexual relations. But as he imagined that might be a bit uncomfortable for her, he showed restraint and uttered, "Let's go to your bedroom."

"Yes, let's…" she agreed, taking him by the hand and leading the way, as they brought the glasses of wine with them.

KENAN FERNÁNDEZ FINALLY decided to drag himself from the Hawthorne Bar and Grill on Burnsten Street before they kicked him out. He finished off the Alabama slammer whiskey shot and headed for the door, still miffed that Nikki Sullivan had decided he wasn't worth her time.

Without even giving him a chance to show what he was truly made of, she'd essentially kicked him to the curb. That included blocking his calls and texts, adding insult to injury. She had apparently taken up with this other dude—a special agent—who had threatened to have him charged with aggravated stalking if he didn't back off his pursuit of Nikki.

Kenan muttered an expletive as he stumbled across the small parking lot toward his red BMW 228i Gran Coupe. He had admittedly never taken rejection well. And he wasn't quite ready to start now. But how could he compete in a fair fight against someone who seemed equally determined to keep him away from the gorgeous woman Kenan had a thing for?

He climbed into the vehicle, buckled up and headed home to the nearby beachfront condominium he owned.

Caught up in his thoughts, Kenan was oblivious to the fact that he was being followed. It was only when another vehicle—a gray Buick Encore—pulled up alongside his on the driver's side with the passenger window rolled down, that he took notice. But by the time Kenan became aware that someone was pointing a gun at him through his own open window, it was too late to do anything about it, as a shot rang out, hitting Kenan squarely in the face.

His world had already gone dark by the time a second shot hit the mark, for good measure. Kenan Fernández's car veered out of control, crashing into a light pole.

The Buick continued on down the street as if nothing tragic had happened.

Chapter Ten

"Do you happen to have any condoms?" Gavin thought to ask Nikki as they stood in her primary bedroom, still fully clothed while they were between hot kisses. She had let down her hair.

She was happy that he was responsible in wanting to protect them from an unplanned pregnancy, but told him to ease his concerns, "I'm on birth control." Nikki added, "But if you'd feel more comfortable using a condom—"

"I'm good," he told her in a relaxed manner, indicating that Gavin was confident that neither of them had any sexually transmitted diseases and was ready to carry on.

"So am I," she let him know coolly, eager to be with him in intimate relations.

"Then let's do this." Gavin put his hands on her cheeks and they started kissing again.

Nikki felt as light as a feather as she inhaled his manly scent and fantasized about what was to come, a decade after her earlier fantasies about him. They pulled apart and stripped off their clothing. It took her only an instant to realize that Gavin's firm body in the nude and rock-hard abs were everything she had imagined and then some.

"You're perfect," she gushed, unable to resist saying it, even while he was perusing her admiringly.

He laughed. "Not sure about that, but I am sure where it concerns just how gorgeous you are from head to toe… and everything in between…"

"Hmm…" Nikki basked in the words every woman wanted to hear before making love. "Come here, handsome—"

Gavin obeyed, gave her a mouthwatering kiss, then scooped her up in his arms and carried her to the bed. Just as Nikki sought to take the lead in their foreplay, he told her smoothly, "Relax. And enjoy this…"

She did as she was told, closing her eyes, when Gavin used his mouth and masterful fingers over the expanse of her entire body to whip Nikki up into a frenzy. Unable to take it anymore, needing him as she had never needed anyone like this, she uttered demandingly, "I want you inside me—now!" She sighed and softened her tone, but not the fervent desire she had. "Please, make love to me, Gavin."

"I'm more than willing to do as you ask," he responded, his voice lowered an octave to reflect his own overpowering needs. "I want you too—more than you could ever know…"

He climbed atop her and Nikki lurched as Gavin plunged deep inside her. She wrapped her long legs around his hard back and moaned as the feeling of sexual satisfaction gripped her like a fever. The instantaneous nature of the climax shocked Nikki in a way, but was quite expected in another, as the pent-up needs were brought to the surface by Gavin and his determination to please.

It was only after this that she gave him the go-ahead to complete their lovemaking by reaching his own apex of fulfillment. Their slickened bodies clung together like second skins as Nikki had a second orgasm and cherished it, before things settled down and they lay side by side on the satin sheet, catching their breaths.

"Did we really just do that?" she had to ask with a nervous laugh while regaining her equilibrium.

He raised a brow. "Uh, if you mean red-hot sex, then the answer is yes, we did."

"Okay." Nikki colored. "I know what transpired—and I agree, it was mind-blowing—but was it because you truly wanted me or someone you could no longer have?" she questioned openly, as Brigette entered her head, perhaps unwisely.

"Definitely you," Gavin made clear, seemingly picking up on the insinuation. "What I had with Brigette was then—painful as it was to deal with her murder while knowing the escaped killer is still on the loose—and this is now and all about us as two people attracted to each other, who needed what happened between us and acted upon it."

She smiled, feeling relieved. "Good answer."

"I meant every word," he assured her. "I'm not looking to go backward in time—only forward to wherever that leads us."

"Me too." Nikki wondered just where that might be. She vowed not to overthink things, such as what would happen after the Perry Evigan episode had ended, and let it play out in real time.

Gavin cozied up to her. "Good. Now that we settled that, might a second round be in the cards?"

She chuckled. "Are you sure you have the energy?"

He laughed. "I think I can manage when I'm with someone who is a total turn-on."

Nikki felt him caressing her, causing her own need for

him to be reinvigorated. "Works both ways," she promised, then upturned her mouth to meet with his in a passionate kiss.

GAVIN TRIED TO sit still on the wooden stool in Nikki's studio the following morning. He had let her talk him into posing for an oil painting. As she had been persistent enough, the least he could do was capitulate and let her go to work, even if he didn't necessarily see himself as worthy of being the subject to be shown in a future art exhibit. Or even hanging on the wall surrounded by an expensive frame. But if Nikki felt otherwise, who was he to argue? Not to mention, he was flattered to be seen in a way beyond his professional life in corrections, zeroing in on his physical appearance that he had grown to take for granted through the years.

His mind shifted to making love to Nikki well into the wee hours of the morning. Gavin knew that she saw him as well in a more carnal sense that delved into both their basic instincts and natural attraction toward one another. He pictured her small but full breasts, taut body and perfect streamlined figure—even her small feet and cute toes did it for him. As did her pleasing scent and the way she laughed and blushed.

It made Gavin imagine what it would have been like had he connected with Nikki on this level a decade ago—instead of Brigette—and been allowed to build a relationship over the years. Maybe they would be married today, with children. How had he missed the boat then in not clearly recognizing what was staring him right in the face?

I was too blinded by my stubbornness to look past Brigette's unwillingness to commit to a serious relation-

ship and my foolish attempts to get her to see things my way, to end things between us and look elsewhere for happiness, Gavin chided himself. But it was well past time to move on from past mistakes, and he had, with Nikki, who had come back into his life and helped him to see the light. Much of which shone all around her.

"You're not too deep in thought over there, are you?" She caught his attention as Nikki stood before the canvas, paintbrush in hand, a little paint having found its way on to her white bib apron.

Snapping to attention, Gavin gave a chuckle, realizing he had been caught in reverie. "You got me," he confessed.

She regarded him curiously. "Care to share?"

"I was just thinking that I'm so glad you reappeared in my life."

"Uh, I think it's the other way around," she said wryly.

"How about both?"

"Deal." Nikki studied her subject. "Any complaints?"

"None whatsoever," he promised her. *Both in and out of bed*, Gavin thought truthfully.

"Me neither." Nikki drew a breath. "Can you turn your head just slightly to the right for me?"

Gavin obeyed, then quipped, "Well, now that you mention it regarding complaints, it's anything but easy trying to stay still or keep the smile off my face when I'm desperate to do just the opposite."

She chuckled. "You're doing just fine. I promise, it won't be too much longer."

"Isn't that what all artists tell their subjects?" he questioned.

"Only the ones who whine too much," she tossed back, causing them both to laugh.

"Point well taken." Gavin made a straight face. "No more whining, I promise."

It was this easygoing banter between them, among other things, such as her beauty and their intimate connection, that told him he wanted her in his life well beyond the time when Gavin's special agent duties had come to an end. Were they on the same wavelength here?

When Nikki's cell phone rang, she took the call and listened in, before her expression changed as she blurted out, "What?" Gavin tried to read between the lines, but waited till Nikki's next words were uttered forlornly. "Thanks for letting me know. Bye, Blair."

"What's up?" Gavin asked immediately, detecting the tension in her posture.

Nikki approached him, looking as if she had seen a ghost, and said tonelessly, "My friend Blair just told me that Kenan Fernández is dead."

"Dead?" Gavin got to his feet, meeting her gaze. "How?"

"He was shot to death while driving in his car," she said, a catch to her voice. "The killer is still at large—"

By the uncertain look in Nikki's eyes, Gavin knew that the murder of Kenan Fernández was for her, just as much as for him, a cause for concern. On its face, this may have been entirely coincidental as it related to Nikki. Or could this be connected in any way to the escaped con who was still on the loose as far as Gavin was aware, and potentially targeting Nikki?

HONESTLY, NIKKI WASN'T quite sure what to think as she sat beside Gavin while he drove them to the Owl's Bay Police Department. Had Kenan, whom she barely knew, been involved with some bad people? Was he targeted accidentally?

Or could Perry Evigan have somehow come after him in some sick form of revenge against her? This admittedly seemed like a hard pill to swallow. After all, how would Evigan have known about her one date with Kenan? Never mind the fact that she had absolutely no interest in the personal trainer. But stranger things had happened, hadn't they?

Of course, to believe any of this would mean that Perry Evigan was actually in Owl's Bay. And not in Indiana. Or wherever.

"You all right over there?" Gavin asked, breaking the silence between them.

"I will be, once we can get to the bottom of Kenan Fernández's murder," Nikki responded forthrightly. "Not that I have any vested interest in his death, per se," she pointed out. "Seriously, I never wanted to see him again—"

"But you didn't want to see him dead either, especially as a homicide victim." Gavin turned onto Vandeer Street. "I get that."

"Do you?" She eyed him, but knew they were very much in tune with one another in terms of the possible nature of the murder that neither could ignore.

"Of course." He drew a breath. "Let's not jump the gun though, in making any assumptions that may fall flat, till we see what the police have to say about Fernández's death."

"All right." Nikki yielded to his rational sense of logic. She glanced out the passenger-side window. Getting flustered over what-ifs would do her no good. And only feed into the paranoia she once had regarding Evigan. She couldn't allow him to play with her psyche again. Not unless there was good cause.

INSIDE THE POLICE STATION, Gavin and Nikki met with the homicide investigator assigned to the case, Brooke Reidel. The fiftysomething, slender detective was blue-eyed and had layered strawberry blond hair in a medium cut.

"Nice to meet you, Agent Lynley, Ms. Sullivan," Brooke told them, as she shook their hands in her corner office and then offered a seat in two faux leather guest chairs next to her L-shaped wood desk. She leaned against it and asked, "You wanted info on the Kenan Fernández case?"

Gavin looked up at her from the chair and replied candidly, "Whatever you can share." Knowing it was an ongoing investigation, he added, "Nikki had a run-in with Fernández yesterday at her art exhibition."

Brooke gazed at her intently. "Did you know the victim?"

"We went out once," Nikki said tartly, fidgeting in the chair. "It was a dead end, as far as I was concerned. But Kenan seemed to believe otherwise. He showed up at my showing at the Owl's Bay Art Gallery."

"So, you're saying Fernández was stalking you?"

Nikki glanced at Gavin and back. "Yes, it seemed that way."

"I confronted Fernández at the exhibit and told him to lay off—threatening to have him charged with aggravated stalking," Gavin told her. "Fernández left at that point."

"And you never saw him again?" the detective asked, shifting her eyes from one to the other.

"No, and we were together till this morning." Gavin was more than willing to acknowledge their involvement with one another as their alibi, realizing that the encounter with Fernández technically made them suspects in his murder.

"Okay." Brooke took a breath. "From what we know thus far, last night, Kenan Fernández was at the Hawthorne Bar and Grill on Burnsten Street, before leaving at approximately ten p.m. Shortly thereafter, he was shot to death in his BMW by someone in another vehicle on Shaw Boulevard. We currently have a BOLO alert out for that vehicle, which is believed to be a gray Buick Encore, that was picked up on surveillance video around the estimated time the incident occurred."

"What can you tell us about the weapon used to kill Fernández?" Gavin asked her with interest.

"According to the medical examiner and ballistics, the victim was shot twice with 9mm Luger ammo that came from a SIG Sauer P365 9mm pistol," the detective said. She added, "Our Crime Scene Investigations Unit was able to collect the shell casings near the crime scene to corroborate this finding." She gazed at Gavin. "Why do you ask?"

"Nikki was a witness and the victim of an escaped serial killer, Perry Evigan," Gavin told her, glancing at Nikki, whose shoulders slumped understandably. "One of the weapons Evigan and his fellow escapees stole was a SIG Sauer P365 9mm handgun," he recalled, making him fearful that Evigan could be in Owl's Bay.

Brooke reacted to this revelation by creasing her brow. "Yeah, I heard about Evigan's escape and the farmhouse fire that took the lives of the other two fugitives and another ex-con." She eyed Nikki. "Sorry you were put through that. It must have been awful."

"It was," she confessed. "But that was a long time ago.

I'm over it." Nikki sighed. "Or at least I was, before Evigan broke out of prison—"

"I get that," Brooke said sympathetically. "But from what I've gathered, Perry Evigan has gotten out of Mississippi."

"We'd like to believe that," Gavin said musingly. "However, given that Fernández was shot with the same type of pistol that Evigan may have in his possession, along with his unnatural desire to go after the only victim to survive his serial murders, I'm not prepared to leave anything off the table where Evigan is concerned."

Nikki's voice shook when she uttered, "I'm a bit spooked as well with the prospect that he might have murdered Kenan as some sort of psycho calling card to let me know he's back and coming for me…"

"I understand both of your concerns," Brooke told them. "It's certainly worth checking out. But we think that Fernández's death may be related to a drug deal gone bad."

Gavin cocked a brow. "Really?"

"Yes. The Hawthorne Bar and Grill has been a hot bed for drug use and trafficking in recent years," the detective said, leaning forward. "Moreover, a witness reported seeing Fernández having a heated exchange with an African American male, described as being in his mid- to late-twenties, shortly before Fernández left the bar. For now, this unidentified male is our primary person of interest."

"All right." Gavin had heard enough. He looked at Nikki and could see her strained features relax with the prospect that Fernández had been murdered by someone other than Perry Evigan. This too gave Gavin comfort, as the last thing he wanted was for the serial killer fugitive to have tracked Nikki down, with sure intent to do her bodily harm. He stood, prompting her to do so as well. "Thanks for your time," he told the detective.

Brooke nodded. "I know the BOLO for Perry Evigan is still in effect, as long as he remains free. If we get any credible information that suggests he has come to this town, you can be sure that the Mississippi Department of Corrections will be informed, Agent Lynley."

Gavin offered her a small grin. "Fair enough."

They walked out of the Owl's Bay Police Department with a renewed sense of safety. But in the back of his mind, Gavin still had an uneasy feeling that danger could well lurk around one corner or another as he knew there would be no rest as long as the Gulfport Nightmare Killer remained on the loose somewhere.

Chapter Eleven

Nikki was happy to resume the portrait of Gavin, if for no other reason than to take her mind off the unexpected death of Kenan Fernández. It may have been a big mistake when she agreed to go out with him, and he could be a real jerk in his persistence, but he certainly didn't deserve to die. Even if he was into drug dealing, as the police suspected, which she still found hard to believe. It seemed to her that, as a personal trainer, he prided himself on staying healthy and fit. Neither went well with drug use, which often accompanied those who were in the business of trafficking drugs. But what did she know?

"Now, if you could just bend your head ever so slightly to the left, that would be perfect," she told Gavin, who complied with a handsome grin playing on his nice lips. He was not only an excellent subject, with great bone structure and a flawless complexion, but he also didn't complain like some of her other subjects. Come to think of it, he checked a lot of the boxes for her—not only as ideal for painting, but as great relationship material as well. Not to mention, he was a good lover whom she could never imagine tiring of.

"If there's anything else I can do to make your job easier, just say the word," Gavin told her smoothly.

"Hmm..." Nikki flashed her teeth with a naughty thought. *Be careful what you agree to*, she mused. "I'll certainly keep that in mind." She worked on his gray eyes with her brush, feeling that they were something she could drown in, so enchanting they were. Her thoughts turned back to the murder of Kenan and how relieved she was that apparently this was not the work of Perry Evigan. So why did she still feel uneasy? As if his presence still loomed large? *Get your mind off this and focus*, she admonished herself, peering at Gavin, not wanting to allow her victimizer to ruin a good thing they had going. For however long it lasted.

"So, how are we looking over there?" Gavin asked patiently, his hands resting on his lap.

"Just about done," Nikki told him as she applied the finishing touches around the eyes, before changing brushes to work a bit more on his chiseled chin. "Hope you like it..."

"How can I not?" he expressed confidently. "I've seen your artwork. I'm more than honored to become a permanent part of it."

She blushed. "I'm equally honored that you agreed to sit for me." Not to mention break the ice in coming to her rescue with an escaped killer on the loose. "There," she voiced. "Done, save for a few touch-ups here and there once it dries. Come have a look."

"All right." Gavin got up, stretched his long legs and came over to her.

Nikki waited with bated breath to see what he thought, as he stared at the painting in utter silence. "Well... What do you think?" she asked nervously.

"I love it!" he declared. "You've done an incredible job in capturing the best parts of me."

"You think?" She smiled.

"Unquestionably. I never thought I could look so good on canvas. But you've made a believer out of me, Nikki."

She flushed. "Glad you approve."

He grinned at her. "Oh, I approve of a lot of things about you, Ms. Sullivan."

Her lashes fluttered coquettishly. "Is that so?"

"Yeah." Gavin wrapped his arms around her waist and drew her close. "Such as the sweet taste of your lips."

"Hmm..."

"Mind if I try them on for size?"

"Be my guest." She happily gave in to him.

They kissed for what seemed like a few minutes that definitely left Nikki all hot and bothered, before coming up for air. "I'd better get cleaned up," she told him, knowing she had managed to get paint on her face and hands.

"Okay, if you insist." He favored her with a sexy grin. "But just for the record, even with a few smudges, you still look great."

She laughed. "I'll take your word for that." Along with reading between the lines, which Nikki admittedly felt gave her hope for bigger and better things with him down the line. She headed upstairs to wash her face.

GAVIN WATCHED HER leave the studio, then he turned back to the portrait of himself. He really did appreciate it and wondered if it would find its way into her next art exhibition, before he could take it home. Actually, truth be told, he would rather bring Nikki back to his place, see how comfortable she felt there and see which way the wind blew in enabling them to seize this point in time for establishing a real romance. *Let's see if she's amenable to that when this Evigan business is behind us*, Gavin told himself with optimism, before removing the cell phone from his khaki pants.

He checked his messages and saw a text from Marvin Whitfield, who was following up on their earlier conversation regarding the current whereabouts of Perry Evigan, which made Gavin nervous. He called the director with a video request and asked tentatively after Whitfield accepted it, “So, where do things stand with Evigan?”

Whitfield’s brow furrowed. “We seem to have lost track of his possible whereabouts at the moment,” he said disappointedly. “There’ve been a few sightings here and there, but nothing that has been substantiated.”

“What about the last known vehicle Evigan was believed to be driving?” Gavin thought about the gray Buick Encore that the unsub in Kenan Fernández’s murder may have been driving.

“That’s just it,” the director said, “we don’t have a credible lead on that right now. Could be that he’s driving around in a stolen car that had already been stolen by someone else. Hence, no report of it. If I had to make a guess, I’d say that Evigan is probably changing vehicles every chance he gets—trying to remain one step ahead of the law.”

Gavin didn’t disagree with that assessment. It still left open the door that Evigan could have shown up in Owl’s Bay and was able to locate Nikki, while waiting for the right time and place to strike. He brought up the SIG Sauer P365 9mm pistol that was used to pump two rounds into Fernández’s head. “Could be the same SIG Sauer firearm Evigan stole in Boyle from Donald Takeuchi,” Gavin pointed out.

"Yeah, we're checking into that," Whitfield told him. "We've asked the Owl's Bay Police Department to submit the firearm casings to the National Integrated Ballistic Information Network to see if any matching bullets have been used and, if so, where. Of course, getting ahold of the murder weapon would be very helpful if we're to link the homicide to Evigan."

"I know." Gavin resigned himself to the fact that without possession of the SIG Sauer P365 9mm pistol—in the absence of a positive identification of Perry Evigan in Owl's Bay—he couldn't know for sure if Evigan was the shooter. Or if, in fact, it was a drug-related hit and a local unsub actually carried it out.

"Is she doing okay?" the director asked.

"Nikki's holding up fine," Gavin said, but knew there were limits as to how long that would last. He was glad that Nikki had her art to keep her preoccupied while Evigan continued to elude authorities.

After ending the video chat, in which Whitfield made no mention of withdrawing him from the assignment for now, Gavin gazed again at his oil portrait. He used the cell phone to take a picture of it and then sent it to his sister, followed by his cousins, knowing that they would all enjoy seeing it. If he had his way, Gavin hoped that someday they would all be able to sit for their own portraits. This, of course, would mean that he and Nikki's relationship had become just that—evolving into something that would warrant get-togethers both ways with his family. As well as hers.

On Monday afternoon, Nikki drove to teach her art class at Owl's Bay Community College. Gavin came along for the ride, sitting in the passenger seat, looking at his cell phone. Neither had brought up Perry Evigan today, but she was certain that Gavin was mindful that the serial killer had still not been brought to justice and, consequently, they would remain on edge till such time.

She glanced at Gavin and couldn't help but wonder what his thoughts were for their future. Or had he given much thought at all to whether or not what they had between them was lasting? As opposed to taking a wait-and-see attitude? She wouldn't push him one way or the other—even if in her heart, Nikki knew that what she was starting to feel for Gavin was very real. And not at all subject to misconception. Or time-limited. But that was just her. He would need to decide for himself if he wanted a life with her firmly planted in it or not.

She pulled off Praceson Road and into the parking lot, where Nikki found a spot right in front of the Department of Fine Arts and Design. "Here we are," she told Gavin with a smile.

He looked at her and grinned. "Let's go."

They went inside the building, where Nikki's class was on the first floor. "You're welcome to come in, if you like," she invited Gavin, though suspecting he would decline.

"Thanks, but I'll wait out in the hall," he said. "I need to make some calls and give you your space at the same time. At least in the classroom."

Nikki would have been just as comfortable to have him in her space, but understood that he needed his own, while remembering that he was still on duty as a special agent and surveillance was part of that. So long as Evigan remained even the slightest threat.

"All right." Nikki smiled again at Gavin. "See you in

a bit." Carrying a black leather satchel with art materials, she headed inside where students awaited her. She greeted them, including her newest student, Miriam Broderick, who walked up to her, and also happened to be a member of Nikki's support group. It was there that Miriam expressed a strong interest in developing her art skills and working her way past the tragic death of her brother a year ago.

"Hey, Nikki." She flashed a generous smile. "Thanks so much for inviting me."

Nikki's eyes lit up. "Thank you for wanting to come. Hopefully, you'll get what you need to improve your craft and I'll be here to help in any way I can."

"I appreciate that and I'm excited about the opportunity."

"Me too." Nikki grinned and walked toward a kidney-shaped laminate table, where she set the satchel and eyed various works of art lining the walls, and imagined others yet to come, before turning to the students to begin the class.

"I HAVE NEWS..." Jean O'Reilly told Gavin over the phone.

"Hopefully, it's good news," he said, while moving farther down the hall, away from Nikki's classroom.

"I wish," she moaned. "Two days ago, there was an unauthorized use of an ATM card in a town about a hundred and fifty miles from Owl's Bay. This led to a welfare check of the card owner, a fifty-five-year-old male veterinarian named Richard Pelayo. He'd been stabbed to death in his garage. The medical examiner believes Pelayo was killed at least twenty-four hours before his body was discovered."

"And this relates to Evigan how?" Gavin asked tensely.

"A man fitting his general description, and wearing a

hoodie, was picked up on surveillance video outside the house," Jean replied matter-of-factly. "We're still trying to determine if it was Evigan or not by finding his DNA or fingerprints at the crime scene, or other means of identification."

Gavin swallowed thickly, switching the phone to his other ear. "Do you happen to know if Pelayo owned a car?"

"A Buick Encore was registered in his name," she responded. "We think it was stolen by whoever killed Pelayo—"

Gavin frowned. "It's the same make and model as a car involved in the shooting death of a man named Kenan Fernández here in Owl's Bay," he told her bleakly. "If Evigan is the man in the surveillance video footage, then he's likely responsible for both deaths."

"Hmm..." Jean hummed. "I can understand killing Pelayo in the course of a home invasion, but why Fernández?"

"It may have something to do with his interest in Nikki," Gavin said, and explained the convoluted scenario.

"Wow," she voiced afterward. "Seems like a stretch, insofar as motivation. Not to mention the high risk versus uncertain reward for Evigan, should he have been able to fit these pieces together in Nikki's life and times."

"I agree," Gavin told her, when it was put that way. "Maybe I have it all wrong about Perry Evigan. But my gut instincts tell me that I can't rule out anything in regard to what the escaped serial killer may be capable of. Which is why we need to find him ASAP."

"We're doing everything in our power to do just that," Jean assured him. "The Fugitive Apprehension Strike Team and our partners in law enforcement are all over this, looking at every lead regarding Evigan, whether he's still in the state or elsewhere."

"All right." Gavin took a breath. "Let me know what forensics comes up with on the Pelayo murder crime scene or otherwise."

"I will." She paused. "You'll get through this. So will Nikki Sullivan."

"Yeah. I hope you're right." After disconnecting, Gavin walked back toward Nikki's art class and peeked in the door window. He could see her. The need to protect her from the likes of Perry Evigan was stronger than ever. As were the feelings for Nikki that had begun to fill Gavin's heart in ways he couldn't have imagined just a few short days ago. Now it was something he would never want to turn his back on, no matter where things went with them.

He stepped away from the door and called Detective Brooke Reidel, informing her about the possible connection between the murders of Kenan Fernández and Richard Pelayo, with the potential common denominator being wanted fugitive, Perry Evigan.

PERRY HAD ADMITTEDLY grown restless in his intense desire to pick up where he left off as a heartless strangulation serial killer. Time had only increased his appetite for death of those deserving. Though he knew without question that the big prize would be Nikki Sullivan, he had been unable to get to her just yet, thanks to the presence of her bodyguard. Perry assumed he was law enforcement in some capacity, determined to keep Nikki alive.

This was the polar opposite of Perry's own quest and desire. He had waited this long; he could wait a little longer to achieve his ultimate objective. In the meantime, he needed a warm-up to get him back in the game in a way that could get him excited. And he had already latched on to the perfect target for his deadly craving. Now it was just a matter of luring her into his trap, for which there would be no escape.

Tilting the brim of the beige bucket hat he was wearing to help disguise his identity, along with dark cat-eye sunglasses and the stubble he'd allowed to grow on his face and neck, and a fresh set of clothing and boots, Perry walked inconspicuously away from the Owl's Bay Community College's Department of Fine Arts and Design building. Shortly, he arrived at the latest vehicle he had stolen—a blue Toyota Corolla Cross—having believed that the Buick Encore had become too hot now.

Climbing inside, he drummed his fingers on the steering wheel fretfully and waited.

Chapter Twelve

"Mom, Dad, this is Gavin Lynley," Nikki introduced him to her mother and stepfather, Dorothy and William McElligott, via a video chat while holding a tablet in the living room. They were back in Clarksdale after their visit to the Cayman Islands. Now seemed as good a time as any to have them meet Gavin, knowing the bad blood that had once existed between her and Brigette's former boyfriend. So much had changed since then—as it related to Nikki's evolving relationship with the handsome special agent—that it was incumbent upon her to share this with those she was closest to.

"Hi, Gavin," her parents spoke in unison in friendly voices.

"Hey." He looked over Nikki's shoulder. "Good to meet you both."

"You too," her mother said, smiling.

"Same here," her stepdad added, and after a beat, asked, "So, where do things stand on Perry Evigan? I've heard conflicting stories on his whereabouts and even whether or not he's still alive—"

So have I, Nikki thought unnervingly, while considering the latest news that the escaped serial killer may have been involved in an identity theft and home invasion turned deadly in a town a hundred and fifty miles away. The suspect's head was covered with a hood, but he seemed to match Evigan's description and apparently stole the victim's Buick Encore—the same type of vehicle believed to have been used by someone in the murder of Kenan Fernández. Were the culprits truly one and the same? Had her tormentor finally found her?

Gavin, who had managed to keep her grounded while doing his best to downplay the threat, even while being much more guarded against being confronted by the fugitive, responded candidly, "I believe Evigan is still alive. As to his whereabouts, we haven't been able to pinpoint this definitively as yet, but we're working night and day to apprehend him."

Dorothy frowned. "After what that man put my daughter through, I worry that the longer he remains on the loose, the greater the chance that he will find his way back to her for more terrorizing…and worse…"

"I will not let Evigan hurt your daughter," Gavin said firmly, trying to reassure her. "I'm not letting Nikki out of my sight till Evigan is back in custody. Or dead, so he can't ever come after her again."

"Listen to Special Agent Lynley," William said comfortingly to his wife. "Nikki's in good hands. He won't let anything bad happen to her."

"I do feel safe with Gavin nearby," Nikki pitched in, flashing him a smile of support, while knowing that the nature of their involvement had gone well beyond potential victim and protector. "Wherever Perry Evigan is, he's running out of time to remain free. We're okay here."

Her mother's blue eyes crinkled. "I'm happy to know that."

"Love you both," Nikki uttered sweetly, promising to keep them abreast of anything new to report about the wanted escapee. Beyond that, she was eager to apprise them of where things were headed between her and Gavin, once Nikki knew herself in no uncertain terms.

After ending the video conversation, she gazed at Gavin, who grinned back and said thoughtfully, "Hope I made a good impression on your folks."

"You did," she said knowingly. "I'm sure they approve of you being here."

"Yeah?"

"Of course." She smiled, reflective. "If you get to meet them in person, they will surely fall head over heels for you." *Just as I have*, Nikki told herself.

Gavin blushed. "In that case, I look forward to getting together with your mom and stepdad. And for what it's worth, if my parents were still alive, they definitely would have been happy to meet you and get to know you as someone who's in my life. I'm sure Lauren and her family will be quite taken with you when they get to meet you."

"It's nice to know you feel that way." Even more comforting to Nikki was hearing him say that she was in his life—and wanted to extend that to those he was closest to—giving them both something to build upon.

The trick though, was to not allow Perry Evigan to find a way to come between them as someone who still wanted to see her dead.

AFTER HER OFFICIAL shift had ended on Monday evening, Detective Brooke Reidel received the call that an adult female had been found deceased under highly suspicious circumstances at a residence on Willow Lane. Knowing that her job for the Owl's Bay PD didn't give her the luxury of picking and choosing hours that worked best, Brooke grabbed her Glock 26 Gen5, holstered it and left her dog, an Irish Setter named Mandy, in their Craftsman bungalow, and hopped into her white Ford Explorer to head to the scene.

En route, Brooke got more info on what she was coming upon. According to a first responder, the dead female had been identified by her townhouse neighbor as Miriam Broderick, a twenty-seven-year-old product line supervisor for a trucking company and divorcée who lived alone. Brooke couldn't help but wonder about the other aspects of the victim's life that led up to it ending prematurely. Was it a happenstance victimization? Wrong place, wrong time-type circumstance? Or a terrible situation she put herself in by bad choices or a misguided association?

Truth was that Brooke had seen them all. Even in a relatively small town like Owl's Bay, where she had put in more than twenty years as a detective and more than a decade in homicide. Take, for instance, the death of Kenan Fernández two nights ago. It had all the earmarks of a drug hit. Except for the fact that Fernández was not a known player in the drug use and drug dealing sphere. Nor did he have a criminal record to suggest he was involved in this illicit activity.

On the other hand, Fernández had been accused of stalking. Had that been a factor in his death, as the search continued for the gray Buick Encore believed to have been used in his execution, as well as trying to track down the current person of interest in the case?

Complicating matters was the possibility that the vehicle was stolen and Fernández's killer might be responsible for the murder of another man a hundred and fifty miles away. Brooke considered that the unsub could well be fugitive serial killer Perry Evigan. Nikki Sullivan had managed to come away alive from her ordeal with him, after being drugged and kidnapped by Evigan. Had he shown up in Owl's Bay to take another crack at her?

Brooke left that one to ponder as she pulled up to the Cetona Townhomes complex on Willow Lane. After getting out of her car and bypassing onlookers, in what had clearly become a crime scene, she ducked under the yellow tape and made her way up the stairs to the victim's townhouse, where Brooke was greeted in the foyer by Officer Lester Hu. She flashed her identification at the twentysomething, slender Asian man, who was brown-eyed and had black hair in a faux hawk style, and asked him routinely, "What do we have?"

Lester furrowed his brow. "It looks to be a homicide," he spoke bluntly. "It's not pretty. See for yourself." He turned away from her.

Brooke stepped inside the contemporarily furnished great room and saw that it had been ransacked. Lying face up on the bamboo floor behind a coffee-colored love seat with flared arms was the nude body of an adult female with short, choppy brown hair with blond streaks. Her green-brown eyes, wide-open, were devoid of any signs of life. A scarf was wrapped tightly around her neck in a way that made it clear that this was no fashion statement.

A chill ran through Brooke as her mind went straight to the so-called Gulfport Nightmare Killer—whose calling card in a series of ligature strangulations included a scarf asphyxiation. Was he back in business—only now as the Owl's Bay Nightmare Killer?

GAVIN GOT A phone call from Detective Brooke Reidel. He assumed she had an update on the unsub and/or vehicle believed to have been used in the deadly attack on Kenan Fernández. Knowing that Nikki would want to hear this too, and feeling a need to keep her informed, he put it on speakerphone—even if he would rather shield her from any unsettling news pertaining to Perry Evigan. Especially with the promise made to her mom and stepdad about protecting their daughter at all costs. It was something Gavin stood by, as much for his own desire for a long-term future with Nikki in it, as doing right by Nikki and her folks.

"Detective Reidel," Gavin said apprehensively. "What do you have for me—or us?" he amended as he let her know she was on speaker, and gazed at Nikki, as they stood inside her art studio.

"I'm afraid it's not good…" Brooke sighed. "I'm at the scene of a homicide. The white female victim, age twenty-seven, was found by a neighbor. In a preliminary examination, the Yaeden County medical examiner believes that the decedent, Miriam Broderick, was strangled to death with the scarf wrapped around her neck…"

"Did you say Miriam Broderick?" Gavin asked, recognizing the name.

"Yes—do you know her?"

He turned to Nikki, whose expression dampened as she responded solemnly, "Miriam was in my support group for trauma survivors. She also attended an art class I taught today at Owl's Bay Community College." Nikki's voice shook as she asked the detective timorously, "Do you think this was the work of Perry Evigan?"

Brooke wasted no time in replying straightforwardly, "It fits the MO of Evigan's previous strangulation murders. Of course, we won't know for certain till we see if his DNA or fingerprints were left at the crime scene," she emphasized. "We're looking at surveillance video as well."

Nikki's eyes narrowed. "If it was Evigan, then he knows where I am and will try to come after me," she argued.

"If Evigan wanted to announce his presence, all he's done was bring more heat on him," Gavin stressed, placing his hand on the small of her back supportively.

"Agent Lynley is right," Brooke said firmly. "We'll be working overtime to solve Ms. Broderick's murder—whoever the perp is…"

"Anything more on the gray Buick Encore?" Gavin asked the detective. With its possible connection to the murders of Kenan Fernández and Richard Pelayo, there was also good reason to link the vehicle to Perry Evigan, now the chief suspect in yet another homicide.

"We're still trying to locate the vehicle," she told him, sounding irritated. "It's only a matter of time before we do, then we'll have a better idea of where we stand on the multiple investigations."

Gavin gritted his teeth. "Keep me posted."

"Of course," she promised. "In the meantime, we can put patrols around Ms. Sullivan's house, if you like?"

"Sounds like a great idea," he responded, but knew that this might still not be sufficient, if Evigan was intent on coming after her.

Once Gavin was off the phone, he faced Nikki, who uttered with watery eyes, "If Miriam was killed because of me—"

"You weren't responsible for her death, no matter who the killer was," he wanted to make clear, even if Gavin knew how easy it was for Nikki to blame herself, were

Evigan behind it. "There was no way for you to know that Evigan would break out of prison and find a way to remain on the loose for days—killing anyone who stood in his path. Or otherwise, was ripe for the picking."

"You're right." She twisted her lips acquiescently. "But that doesn't make me feel a whole lot better."

"Come here." He brought her up to his chest, wrapping his arms around her. "You'll get past this, Nikki," he promised. "We both will."

In that instant, Gavin couldn't help but think about Brigette and how—through fate, by design, or whatever—her tragic death had brought him and Nikki together and given them a chance to come to terms with the past and see the light that a future could bring them. So long as the darkness of an escaped serial killer didn't snuff it out.

IN SPITE OF a mostly restless night's sleep, for all the wrong reasons, Nikki was up bright and early the next morning. She was still trying to square with the reality that her fellow survivor of a traumatic time and art student, Miriam Broderick, was a victim of a homicide. What was that all about? *Was she targeted because of me?* Nikki had to wonder, even when she knew that things did happen in life or the universe itself happenstance, with no one at fault, per se.

On the other hand, she knew that someone was most definitely at fault for Miriam's death. Was it Perry Evigan? Or someone else as perhaps payback for a drug deal gone bad?

As she wrestled with these thoughts, Nikki found Gavin sitting at the breakfast nook table, gazing at his computer. Beside him was a mug of hot coffee. He looked up at her and grinned, giving her the once-over, as she'd thrown on one of his button-down shirts—it was light green and oversize on her, but surprisingly comfortable. "Hey," he said.

"Hi." She blushed under his perusal.

"I don't imagine you slept much better than I did."

"I think you're right."

"Sorry about that." Gavin furrowed his brow. "Coffee's ready."

"Thanks." Nikki was happy that he seemed to have made himself quite at home in her kitchen and elsewhere. Sign of the times? Or future? She poured herself a cup of coffee and studied him, fully dressed for the day. "What are you doing?" Her voice rang with curiosity, knowing the uneasiness in the air with the latest revelations.

He hesitated. "I was just taking a look at the autopsy report on Miriam Broderick."

Nikki cringed while imagining her horrific death. "What were the results?" she asked, taking a seat across the table on the side bench.

"I'll spare you the details," he said protectively.

"Don't." She peered at him. "I'm a big girl, Gavin. I also witnessed firsthand someone being strangled." Brigette's once beautiful face appeared in Nikki's head, before it was forever tarnished by that maniac. "If this is the work of Perry Evigan, I need to know what he's up to, no matter the chilling nature of it…"

"All right." Gavin nodded understandingly. He took a breath, glanced at the screen and stated, "According to the Yaeden County Medical Examiner Flora Ueoka, Miriam was the victim of ligature strangulation, with the actual cause of death being asphyxia. She was also sexually assaulted by her killer…" Gavin paused and gazed at Nikki. "Do I need to go on…?"

"No." She'd heard enough and did not need more explicit information from the report on the suffering Miriam had been put through, before death came mercifully. Nikki sighed and asked pointedly, "Do you think it was him?"

Gavin tasted his coffee musingly and responded with candidness, "We need to be prepared for that distinct possibility."

Her eyes grew wide and her mouth hung open distraughtly. "How does one prepare for the reality that a monster is out there—back in force in picking and choosing which women to rape and strangle to death next?"

Reaching out and taking her hand, Gavin said composedly, "By steeling ourselves against falling into his trap of feeling helpless. Or a bad sense of inevitability. Wherever this thing goes, we control our own destiny. I'll be damned if I allow Evigan to dictate that for you or me. And I won't let you feel that way either."

Nikki wrapped her fingers around his large hand, with her pulse racing, but her heart telling her that having him on her side was more than she could ask for against a common enemy. Even if Perry Evigan was not the one responsible for Miriam's death, his sheer presence as an escaped serial murderer could not be dismissed. So long as the menace of him remained a serious thorn in Nikki's side for her health, well-being and longevity.

Chapter Thirteen

Gavin watched as Nikki headed upstairs to get dressed. If he had his way, he'd love to see her completely undressed and spend as much time as possible with her in bed. She had that kind of effect on him these days. Probably would have a decade ago as well, had he given her half a chance instead of his misguided belief that Brigette was *the one*. Clearly, she was not. He had already come to that painful realization, more or less, when she was killed. But by then, it was too late in the game to see if he and Nikki might have made a connection before someone else won her heart.

This is a whole new beginning for us, Gavin thought, tasting his second cup of coffee. He could live with that and see where it went. All that mattered for the time being was that they couldn't allow Perry Evigan to put a halt to their progress by victimizing Nikki as he wanted to do, in following what he did to Brigette.

Gavin phoned Brooke Reidel for a video chat as he paced around between the living and dining areas, returning her call from a couple of minutes earlier. When her face appeared on the cell phone screen, he said cautiously, "Hey. What's up?"

"We located the gray Buick Encore linked to the murder of Kenan Fernández," Brooke said, running a finger across a thin brow. “It was abandoned behind a vacant building on Tuffas Road. We dusted it for prints and were able to retrieve some that belonged to Evigan. He was definitely in that car at some point,” she stated matter-of-factly. “And he has to be considered the number one person of interest in the murder of Kenan Fernández.”

Gavin jutted his chin and, before she could continue, asked her, “What about the Buick itself—was it…?”

“Yes, the car belonged to Richard Pelayo,” Brooke confirmed. “As such, there’s every reason to believe that Evigan killed him too, before taking his car and driving it a hundred and fifty miles to Owl’s Bay to continue the murder spree…”

As Gavin digested this, it left the obvious question in his head and the anticipated answer. “Are you saying what I think you are regarding the death of Miriam Broderick?”

Brooke furrowed her brow and nodded affirmatively. “DNA removed from the victim as a result of being sexually assaulted was sent to CODIS. It came back with a match of Perry Evigan’s DNA. Moreover, his fingerprints were also left at the scene of the homicide, leaving little doubt that he murdered Ms. Broderick and is still at large.”

“And coming after Nikki.” Gavin uttered what the detective was surely thinking.

“We’ve alerted the relevant authorities about this and Owl’s Bay is now front and center in the search for the escaped con,” Brooke said with concern in her voice. “In the meantime, the police department will assist in any way we can to keep Ms. Sullivan—Nikki—safe.”

“All right.” After he ended the call, while considering his options and waiting for Nikki to come down, Gavin wasted little time in phoning Marvin Whitfield to confer on the news that Perry Evigan was almost certainly still in Owl's Bay and, as such, a clear and present danger to Nikki.

Whitfield muttered an expletive and snorted, "How this bastard has managed to evade the law while resuming his murderous ways is beyond me."

"I'm in total agreement," Gavin told the director respectfully, in assessing Evigan's amazing ability to dodge recapture and add more notches to his belt as a serial killer and sociopath, "but that doesn't change the fact that by his mere presence in town, Evigan is threatening the very person you assigned me to protect. That's problematic, to say the least."

"I hear you." Whitfield took a breath. "So, what do you suggest?"

"I need to move Nikki out of Owl's Bay, to be on the safe side." Gavin took nothing away from the ability of the MDOC's Fugitive Apprehension Strike Team and other law enforcement agencies involved in the hunt for Evigan. Or, for that matter, the benefits of sheltering in place at the cottage with a good security system and him being armed. With the Owl's Bay PD providing adequate backup. But honestly, none of that gave Gavin comfort right now that the escaped killer might not still find a way to breach that safety net and place Nikki in harm's way.

I couldn't live with myself if I let Evigan have a repeat performance in victimizing Nikki again, Gavin thought, determined not to let that happen. He hoped the director was on board with this.

"Where to?" Whitfield asked.

"A lakefront cabin in the woods just outside of Gulfport," he said to him. "A friend of mine named Jake Kendrick owns it. I've spent time there. It's secluded and has plenty of windows to give me a 360-degree view of who's coming and going. I'm sure he won't mind letting us borrow it for a day or two, if necessary, while Evigan is being tracked down and ultimately taken into custody."

"Okay, then go for it," the director said. "If you're sure about this?"

"I'm just going with my gut here," Gavin told him frankly. "I think it's better to err on the side of caution by temporarily relocating Nikki." The thought had crossed his mind about taking her back to his house in Jackson as a safe refuge. But given the distance and high likelihood that Evigan would be recaptured shortly, Gavin opted against making a move that might seem a bit premature and presumptuous as it related to things evolving in their personal relationship sooner than Nikki might have desired. The last thing he wanted was to rush her. Or otherwise mess things up between them by jumping the gun. "Having lost someone to Perry Evigan ten years ago, I don't want to give him even the slightest opportunity to come for Nikki again—in a place that he may well have already sized up."

"I understand. Get her out of there, then, Lynley. We'll do everything in our power to recapture Evigan and put him back where he belongs. Hopefully, that will come sooner rather than later. Until then, Nikki Sullivan—and you—deserve some peace of mind while the serial killer remains on the loose."

"Thanks, Director Whitfield." Gavin took a calming breath, but knew there would be no comfort as long as the threat to Nikki's life remained real.

"As an added measure of security, we'll send along a

US marshal to escort you and provide an extra set of eyes for your destination," Whitfield said.

Gavin thanked him again and disconnected, only to find Nikki standing there with a hand on her hip and a scowl on her face.

NIKKI HAD OVERHEARD some of Gavin's conversation with the Director of Investigations at MDOC. They were talking about moving her out of Owl's Bay, to a cabin in the woods, while Evigan remained free and a threat to her life. She cringed at the implications, but needed to get the scoop from Gavin on exactly why she needed to leave the cottage.

"Hey," Gavin said evenly, though his hardened expression gave away the uneasiness he felt about the current situation.

"What is going on?" she asked straightforwardly, peering at him. "Why the need to relocate me…?"

He drew a breath and, meeting her gaze directly, replied in an acerbic tone of voice, "It's been confirmed that Perry Evigan is in Owl's Bay. His DNA was found on Miriam Broderick and his prints were also found at the crime scene…"

Nikki gasped and put a hand to her mouth as the gravity of Evigan doing to Miriam what he did to Brigette hit her like a ton of bricks. Suspecting something was bad enough. Having it verified was so much worse and left Nikki speechless.

Gavin placed his hands on her shoulders and said knowledgeably, "Beyond that, Evigan's prints were also found in a stolen vehicle believed to have been used by the shooter in the death of Kenan Fernández and another man. Why Evigan would go after Fernández is anyone's guess. But I do know that while Evigan is still on the loose, you're not safe here, Nikki." Gavin's warm breath fell onto her face. "I want to take you to a friend's log cabin, where I can put some distance between here and Evigan's reach. Now that his location has been pinpointed, I expect our Fugitive Apprehension Strike Team and supporting law enforcement to close in on him at any time. But even that's not soon enough to want to wait around and give him a target—you."

"I don't want that either," Nikki said in a hushed voice. "I'll go pack some things."

"Good." Gavin flashed her a sideways grin. "Make it quick. We don't want Evigan to have any time to make his move."

She nodded. "Right."

Having Gavin at this cabin with her would certainly make it easier for Nikki to temporarily relocate from what was supposed to be her comfort zone, after leaving Gulfport eight years ago. Now Perry Evigan had managed to turn her world upside down. And make her cottage a place she could not feel safe in while he was on the prowl, having already murdered two people she was acquainted with in Miriam and Kenan.

The last thing Nikki wanted was to join them—and Brigette—in an early grave. But was there truly anywhere that she could escape the serial killer's wrath against her as the sole survivor of his onslaught?

HALF AN HOUR LATER, Nikki was meeting with her friend, Blair Roxburgh, at Calyne's Coffee Café on Foulter Way. She didn't dare go to Blair's house, potentially placing her in danger. But given the murder of Miriam Broderick, Nikki felt a need to reach out to the support group founder before she left town temporarily. A café in a public space made it unlikely that a wanted fugitive would show his face there. If he were to, Gavin, who was seated at another table to give them a little space and trying to keep a low profile while on the lookout for the serial killer, would nab Evigan in a hurry, as per his role as her protector.

Nikki waved Blair over as she spotted her entering the café. The two women hugged and Nikki cried, "I'm so sorry about Miriam."

"So am I," Blair uttered. "She didn't deserve to go that way."

"I know." Nikki pulled away, wiped her eyes and they sat at a square wooden table away from the window, where she had taken the liberty of ordering them both iced lattes and cinnamon rolls. "Perry Evigan killed her."

Blair lifted a brow. "Are you sure about that?"

"I only wish I weren't." Nikki frowned. "It gets worse. The police believe that Evigan killed Kenan Fernández too."

Blair's eyelids fluttered wildly. "What?"

Nikki told her what she knew about the crimes and the massive search for Perry Evigan underway in Owl's Bay. "Seems like he's been fixated on me ever since he escaped from prison, along with anyone I'm associated with..." She glanced over at Gavin, who was shifting his gaze this way and that for any sign of trouble, and turned back to her friend. "I never imagined that—"

"Stop it." Blair leaned forward, touching her hand. "You're in no way to blame for someone else's actions, Nikki. Least of all an escaped serial killer's. The fact that

Perry Evigan has somehow been able to carry out more crimes while on the run is not your fault. You're as much a victim as anyone. But you're also a survivor—and don't ever let him or anyone else take that away from you."

Nikki grabbed a cinnamon roll, nibbled off a piece defiantly and then declared, "I won't." She couldn't give in to Evigan's tactics, even if from a distance. Hadn't the years since the attack made her strong enough to withstand the psychological manipulation? She would not backtrack on that now. Especially with Gavin supporting her. And Blair too. "You're right," she told her. "I can't control what a fugitive serial killer chooses to do, no matter how vile."

"Exactly." Blair favored her with a tiny smile and picked up the latte, taking a sip. She glanced over at Gavin. "Does he want to come and join us?"

"Probably not," Nikki said. "He's fine keeping watch over me while trying not to crowd me. I'm good with that." Not that she had a problem with their spending lots of time together, as they had. The bigger issue still was how they fared once the threat to her life was over, one way or the other.

"Well, I'm glad he's got your back," Blair said. "And I'm sensing it's even more than that."

Nikki blushed. "Let's just say we're in a good place right now."

"Sounds like a nice place to be in."

"It is." She eyed him, and Gavin grinned and lifted his mug of coffee in an approving toast. "But right now, his focus and mine is on averting a confrontation with Perry Evigan. Which is why I'll be leaving town temporarily with Gavin, as the authorities try to close in on Evigan."

"I see." Blair sipped her latte. "I'm sure you feel it's better that I don't know where you're going?"

"Correct—for your own safety," Nikki pointed out, biting off a chunk of the cinnamon roll.

Blair's mouth tightened. "I can take care of myself, always have, ever since the attack back in college," she spoke bravely.

"I know." Nikki understood that, like her, Blair had taken self-defense classes to better protect herself from villains. But even that could only go so far, should the perp catch them off guard. Or otherwise be relentless and lethal in an attack. She smiled at her. "If all goes right, I'll be back before you even start to miss me."

"I'll hold you to that." Blair chuckled, grabbing her cinnamon roll. "In the meantime, let's keep our fingers crossed that the man who ended Miriam's life will be brought to justice in no time flat and you can get back to your life."

Nikki nodded, while crossing her fingers on that thought and hoping for the best, even as something inside her still feared the worst when it came to the maniacal serial killer.

Gavin lifted his mug of flat white coffee and took a sip, as he turned his eyes to Nikki and Blair at their table. He was sure that they were commiserating over the senseless loss of their survivor support group member, Miriam Broderick. Gavin knew that the only way the pain would be eased was with the capture or elimination of the person responsible for her death. Though he was certain that was imminent, and he would like nothing better than to slap the cuffs on Brigette's murderer himself, Gavin's number-one priority had to be protecting Nikki at all costs. He would defer dealing with Perry Evigan to his colleagues.

I need to get her out of here to a safe place where he can't find her, Gavin told himself, assuming Evigan, against all odds, managed to slip past the tracking operation well underway in town. He owed it to her to not give the escaped con an opportunity to replay the terror he'd instilled upon her a decade ago.

Lifting his cell phone, Gavin called his friend, Jake Kendrick. The two had known each other since they attended Mississippi State University and lived in the same residence hall. Jake now lived in Winnipeg, Manitoba, in Canada, where he owned an upscale restaurant and was happily divorced. He kept his cabin as an investment property and for occasional getaways.

Jake accepted the video chat request. Thirty-six, with a medium build and dark hair in a sideswept undercut, and bearing a crooked grin on his round face, he said, "Special Agent Gavin Lynley. What's up, dude?"

Gavin grinned. "I'm good. How about you?"

"Busy as ever. That's the restaurant business for you. No rest for the weary, but I can't complain."

"Then you're in better shape than I am," Gavin said wryly.

"I seriously doubt that," Jake countered. "At least physically speaking."

Not going there, Gavin got to the point. "Say, I have a big favor to ask of you…?"

"Name it."

"I need to borrow your cabin for a day or two—it's important," he emphasized without going into the details. Jake had been there for him during his darkest hours, but now was not the time to relive the past or address the future. "I promise to leave it the way I find it."

"No problem," Jake said without prelude. "It yours for as long as you want. I don't expect to be back in Mississippi for the foreseeable future."

"Thanks. I owe you one," Gavin told him.

"And I won't let you forget it." Jake laughed. "There's some beer in the fridge, but not much else."

"That's a pretty good start," Gavin quipped. "I'll take it from there."

"Cool. And in case you've forgotten, the key is still under the mat."

"I remember."

"Have fun or whatever. Or with whomever."

Gavin smiled, looking at Nikki. He disconnected and briefly thought about Brigette and how the two women were so different. If only he had been able to better read the tea leaves back in the day, he might have been able to save Brigette and build something much sooner with Nikki. But he had now to turn the page and welcomed the opportunity to do so.

He stood and went over to Nikki's table. After acknowledging Blair, he asked Nikki, "Are you ready to go?"

"Yes." She smiled at him and rose. "All set."

Blair got up as well. Putting her hand on Gavin's elbow, she looked him in the eye and said sharply, "Take care of her."

"I will," he promised, while knowing it was something he didn't take lightly. Not by a long shot.

Chapter Fourteen

As Nikki waited in his car for the drive to the cabin, Gavin conferred outside it with the MDOC's Fugitive Apprehension Strike Team Commander, Eddie Prescott, telling him calculatingly, "Evigan's here, lurking in the shadows, daring us to find him and take him down."

Prescott, fortysomething, built like a brick, with graying hair in a buzz cut and a dimpled chin, narrowed his brown eyes and declared decisively, "If he's still in Owl's Bay, we'll find him—one way or the other. You can be sure of that."

Gavin only wished he could be. As it was, the fact that Evigan had skillfully eluded capture thus far, made the escaped serial killer that much more formidable an opponent. "I want to believe you can track him down, once and for all," Gavin told his friend. "With all the manpower we have in the pursuit, along with any help from the public, it should be a given that Evigan's days as a free man are numbered. But if it's all the same to you, I need to put some distance between Evigan and Nikki Sullivan, the one person who came out alive after crossing paths with that monster."

Prescott glanced at Nikki in the Chevy Tahoe and said

understandingly, "Do what you need to do. Keep her safe till this is over."

"I intend to." Gavin shook his hand. "If this goes sour, don't hesitate to reach out to me."

"I won't," Prescott promised. "Now, get out of here."

"Okay."

Gavin walked away and over to the gray Chevrolet Blazer that belonged to US Marshal Everett Ulbricht, who was in the driver's seat. The marshal, who was in his midthirties, was assigned to follow them to the cabin and make sure they weren't being followed or threatened in any other way. He had on a black cap over curly brown hair and wore dark shades.

"Ready to hit the road?" Gavin asked him.

Ulbricht nodded, touching his sunglasses. "Yeah, let's do it."

"Okay," Gavin said, and glanced around before returning his gaze to Ulbricht. "If you see any sign of Evigan—"

"I'll let you know," the marshal told him in earnest.

"All right." Gavin went to his own car and got behind the wheel. He smiled at Nikki, trying to make this seem like a vacation getaway, rather than running and hiding from an escaped convict who had her in his crosshairs. "I think we're good to go now."

"Great." She smiled back, putting up a brave front, masking what Gavin was certain was an uncomfortableness in having her life put on hold. And all because Perry Evigan had not been taken into custody—keeping the danger he presented alive and well.

If there was a silver lining to the dark cloud the serial killer represented, Gavin saw it as another opportunity to bond more with Nikki in a neutral and relaxed woodsy environment. Even if short-lived, it could be just enough to make a difference in what they were starting to feel for one another.

AFTER A LARGELY silent ride down US Route 49 North, Gavin turned onto Blane Lake Street, an unpaved road in Osweka County. He waved at US Marshal Everett Ulbricht, indicating that the marshal was no longer needed as an escort the rest of the way. Nikki watched him give Gavin the thumbs-up and continue down the highway. She felt somewhat relieved that there had been no indication from Marshal Ulbricht that they had been followed from Owl's Bay, suggesting that Perry Evigan had no idea where she'd gone, as the authorities closed in on him.

Driving a short distance past groves of broadleaf and conifer trees, Gavin pulled up to the red log cabin. Nikki took one look at the two-level lakefront property and couldn't help but utter in awe, "When you said your friend had a cabin in the woods, I was just assuming it was a typical campground-type cabin—not this!"

"Yeah, it is pretty cool." Gavin chuckled. "Jake got a good deal on it, borrowing money from his folks to pay for it. Though he's living in Canada now, he wisely decided to hang on to the place, which is a perfect hideaway for us to lay low for a little while. Why don't we go take a look inside?"

"Okay."

Nikki wanted to forget about this being more about Perry Evigan threatening her life than building a future life with Gavin. Or were the two inexorably linked? How could they not be? Hadn't her shared experience with

Gavin led to this point in time, with Brigette's killer still able to effectively mess with their heads?

But the unintended tugging at their heartstrings and what it might foretell was something that Nikki clung to as what she hoped to be the most important thing to come out of this ordeal, whenever it was over.

Upon grabbing their bags, they headed down the stone walkway and onto the wraparound deck, where Nikki watched as Gavin dug the key out from beneath a white-and-black-striped welcome mat and unlocked the door. "Here it is," he said, as they stepped inside.

Setting her things down, Nikki took a sweeping glance of the first level. It had a cathedral ceiling with exposed beams, laminate wood flooring, floor-to-ceiling windows throughout, offering breathtaking views of the lake from different angles, and rustic pine wood furniture. There was a full-size chef's kitchen with granite countertops. And a security system.

"Nice," Nikki had to say, admitting that if she had to relocate temporarily with barely a moment's notice, this might have been the place she would have chosen to be sheltered with Gavin. "Very nice."

"Yeah." He grinned at her. "Want to see the rest?"

"Sure." She followed him up the wooden U-shaped staircase to the second floor and took in the well-appointed main bedroom, with barn-wood furniture and a built-in sunroom. The thought of them making good use later of the rustic king bed excited her. Or did Gavin not have that in mind in his capacity as Special Agent Lynley? "I like the way your friend has decorated the place," she said, sending her thoughts in a different direction.

"Me too."

They finished the tour, which included an upstairs deck with more magnificent views, for which Nikki was glad she had brought along her sketch pad to draw for a future painting, before heading back down to the first level.

Gavin drew her near to him and said, "Sorry to have to pull you away from Owl's Bay and your life, but I prefer to go with the better safe than sorry philosophy than not."

"It's fine," she told him, smiling. "There are worse things in life than having to be tucked away in a lovely cabin by the lake with a wonderful man."

He gazed longingly into her eyes. "I feel the same way—only turning that around to being here with a gorgeous and sexy woman."

"Hmm…" Nikki felt a flutter of desire, but kept it in check. "So, we're even, then?"

"Yeah, you could say that." Gavin flashed her an askew grin. "Better yet, we're compatible in every way that counts, making what we have that much more compelling."

Her lashes fluttered. "You think?"

"Don't you?"

She answered without preface, "Yes, I believe we are very compatible."

"That really seems to fit when it comes to kissing," he told her.

"Oh…?"

"Yeah." He cupped her cheeks and laid one on her lips, as though to prove the point.

Nikki lost herself in the kiss for a long moment, taking her away from the peril that Perry Evigan had brought upon them in forcing them to escape to a place beyond his reach. When Gavin pulled back, he grinned and said lightheartedly, "Proves my point."

She touched her stinging mouth. "Guess it does."

They went into the kitchen, where Gavin opened up the refrigerator and Nikki saw that it was empty, aside from a bottle of ketchup and three bottles of beer.

"Jake wasn't kidding when he said there was nothing here," Gavin remarked musingly. "Even though we're likely only going to be here for a short while, I suppose we should've stopped at what was probably the only grocery store in town that we passed along the way to pick up a few items."

"There was a pizza place across the street from it," Nikki remembered, feeling her stomach start to growl.

"Why don't we head over there now and get what we need to wait this out," Gavin said, closing the refrigerator, "till the threat that Evigan poses has been brought to a close."

"All right." She wondered just how long that would take, wanting this to be over for good, even while she was happy to make the most of the time away with Gavin.

NIKKI WONDERED IF it was her imagination running wild. She could've sworn she saw Perry Evigan peering at her down the aisle at the supermarket. Or at least someone who resembled him. Granted, she hadn't seen Evigan face-to-face in nearly a decade and only had a mug shot and a photograph shown on television that was taken of him from a court hearing a few years ago when he'd gotten into trouble after a prison fight. But the way the man seemed to be looking at her made Nikki uncomfortable, caught her attention and left her shaking.

She turned to Gavin, who was grabbing a bag of potato

chips from the shelf to put in the cart, and said almost in a whisper, "I think Perry Evigan has found us—"

"What?" Gavin tensed and she could see him nearly go for the firearm that was inside his concealed carry holster, tucked within Gavin's waistband.

"At the end of the aisle..." she stammered, bravely angling her eyes in that direction. Only to find him gone.

"No one's there—" Gavin said, gazing in that direction. He faced her. "What makes you think it was Evigan that you saw?"

"It was just his general appearance and the way he seemed to be studying me, as if sizing me up for the kill..." Nikki swallowed the lump in her throat. "Maybe I was mistaken," she suggested, suddenly questioning her own interpretation.

"Maybe, or maybe not..." Gavin pursed his lips thoughtfully. "Wait right here where I can see you..."

"Okay," she obeyed.

Nikki watched as he hurriedly headed down the aisle and past an elderly female shopper. Gavin kept his hand close to his weapon, without removing it. At the end of the aisle, she saw him look in both directions, before quickly making his way back to her. "Stay put," he directed, and went down the other way to the end, where Gavin peered one way, then the other, before rushing back to her and stating evenly, "I didn't see any sign of anyone who resembled Evigan. But that doesn't mean he wasn't there."

Again, having second thoughts, she wondered out loud, "How would he have found us? Even as he was at the same time trying to avoid recapture?"

"Those are good questions, and there are no easy answers." Gavin rubbed his chin while contemplating this.

"My guess is that you saw someone else and thought it could have been Evigan. If he had followed us out of Owl's Bay, I'm pretty sure that either I or Marshal Ulbricht would have noticed a car that was trailing our vehicles."

Nikki wrinkled her nose. "You're probably right," she conceded, feeling foolish in causing him to panic unnecessarily. "Guess I just got spooked for no reason..."

"You had a very good reason for being spooked," Gavin said, wrapping his hands around the cart's handle. "I'll never fault you for that. Let's pay for these items and go get that pizza."

Nikki nodded and they headed down the aisle, still feeling a bit strange about the entire episode, as if there was an itch that wouldn't go away where it concerned the escaped serial killer.

THOUGH GAVIN WAS fairly certain that Perry Evigan had not found their location and was stalking Nikki as a prelude to kidnapping her again, it still made him nervous about the fugitive, while Evigan remained on the loose. The fact that Nikki had been freaked out at the grocery store in what appeared to be an unprovoked and unreal sighting of the escapee, told Gavin, if nothing else, that Evigan still loomed large in her psyche. That was not likely to change for the time being, in spite of them being thirty miles away from Owl's Bay. And presumably far enough from Evigan's crosshairs to be in a safe space.

Still, Gavin found it incumbent upon himself to reassure Nikki that she needn't worry about the serial killer while they were at the cabin. He wanted the worry to fall on his shoulders instead. "Don't let him get to you. Why don't we just try and relax and enjoy this, to the extent possible,"

Gavin told her in a gentle tone as they sat in ladder-back side chairs across a pine solid wood trestle dining table from one another in the cabin, eating pizza with soft drinks.

"I will if you will," Nikki countered, lifting a slice of the pizza topped with cheddar cheese, ground beef, onions and green peppers.

"Deal." He gave her a convincing grin, wanting to shift the mood to one that was more agreeable—as if they were on vacation together, which he hoped to turn this outing into.

"Good." She bit into the pizza. "Mmm, this is delicious."

Gavin took a bite from his own slice and had to concur. "It is." *But not even close to being as delicious as you are to kiss and make love to*, he told himself, knowing it was coming as much from the heart as his libido. He only needed to show her that more and more, so she knew he meant business in wanting what they had to continue to progress into something truly special when this was over.

While Nikki was clearing the table, Gavin checked the windows and front door to make sure they were locked, then went upstairs, where he called Jean O'Reilly for an update on the situation. "Hey."

"Heard you had gotten out of Dodge," she quipped.

"Seemed like the smart thing to do, with Evigan proving to be so difficult to pin down and take into custody," Gavin said honestly.

"You're probably right about that."

"What's the latest on the search for the fugitive?"

"We haven't captured him yet, if that's what you're asking," Jean told him.

"Didn't think you had." Otherwise, Gavin would know that Nikki was finally out of harm's way for the long-term.

"Anything at all I can work with…?" Before she answered, he added ruefully, "Nikki thought she might have seen Evigan at a store in town. Though I never laid eyes on him to confirm this and am thinking it was a case of mistaken identity, I'd like to know that all signs point toward him still being holed up in Owl's Bay…"

"The signs do suggest that to be the case. But we both know they can be misleading at times."

"How so?" he pressed.

Jean paused. "Surveillance video footage from yesterday picked up a man we believe to be Perry Evigan getting into a blue Toyota Corolla Cross outside of a strip mall in town. We got the license plate number and saw that the car had been reported as stolen. Evigan never bothered to switch plates. There's no reason to believe he's not still driving the vehicle—when out on the road at all—and we've issued a BOLO on it and him."

"All right." Gavin hoped they were that much closer to nailing the bastard and putting an end to the nightmare he'd put Nikki through. "If you get anything at all on his whereabouts or his capture—"

"I'll definitely keep you abreast on all fronts," Jean promised him, before Gavin disconnected.

Nikki had come upstairs and regarded him suspiciously. "Everything okay?"

"Yeah," he said in a calm voice. "We're good."

Chapter Fifteen

"I was thinking that we should make the most of this situation," Gavin uttered erotically to Nikki, while resting his hands on her hips as they stood in the main bedroom.

"Oh, really?" Her lashes fluttered coyly. "And just what did you have in mind?"

He grinned, turned on by her in every way. "Well, this..." Gavin kissed her right cheek. "And this..." Next came the left cheek. "And, of course, there's that—" He went for her abundant mouth, and she reciprocated in kind, letting him know she was more than amenable to what he was suggesting.

"I'm all yours, Agent Lynley." Nikki tsked, wrapping her arms around his neck and bringing their mouths together again for a passionate kiss.

"Since you put it that way, let's see what we can do about that," Gavin teased her.

They wasted no time undressing and he took her to bed, getting cozy atop the matelassé bedspread, where Gavin went to work making sure that he tapped into every sensitive spot on Nikki's perfect body and shapely breasts to give her the hands-on treatment she deserved. Only after the undulating tide of satisfaction came for her amid deep sighs and quivering, did he let go and complete the overwhelming joy of their lovemaking. It sent them both to new heights of ecstasy that was only solidified by their circumstances.

Catching his breath as he lay beside her still and slick body, matching his own, Gavin kissed Nikki's soft shoulder and said truthfully, "I wish we'd had the chance to experience this long ago."

"So do I," she cooed, draping a silky-smooth leg across his thigh. "But it wasn't our time then. I guess it is now."

"Yes, I'd say so." Gavin was in complete agreement. He couldn't very well argue with fate as it were. Maybe they weren't meant to be together ten years ago. Or maybe they were, but were prevented from doing so by forces beyond their control. He wouldn't overthink it. Instead, he was grateful that the universe gave them a second opportunity to find each other and they had. If he had his way, they would never let this slip away.

As soon as the danger that Perry Evigan posed had subsided, Gavin wanted nothing more than to work on a future with Nikki. After all, wasn't that to be expected when two people had fallen in love? Not that he could speak for her, but he could for himself. And when she was ready to tell him how she felt, he would be there to listen.

For the moment, all Gavin wanted to do was hold Nikki, listen to their heartbeats synced and see what tomorrow brought in the hunt for a serial killer escapee.

NIKKI IMAGINED THAT she had known from the moment she first saw Gavin Lynley that she had fallen in love with him. She hadn't exactly been in denial about being in touch with her feelings. It was more that she couldn't act on them with Gavin seeming to be totally hooked on

Brigette. Now it was clear that this hadn't been the case. At least not to the extent that he wouldn't have been open to giving someone else a chance.

The problem had been more of going after someone that her best friend was involved with. Nikki would never have tried to come between Brigette and Gavin—no matter the serious cracks in their relationship—as long as they were together. But now, somehow, some way, Gavin had come into Nikki's life a decade later and things had heated up between them, in and out of the bedroom, telling her that what they had was real. And, from her point of view, it had the potential to be lasting, if she was reading Gavin correctly in his body language and mentality. Now, if only they could put the saga of a dangerous serial killer on the prowl in the rearview mirror.

Slipping from beneath Gavin's protective arms as the morning sun filtered in the window above the cellular shades, Nikki allowed him to get a bit more shut-eye, as she got up and left the room quietly. She hoped to take advantage of this time of the day to sketch the magnificent landscape and breathe in the fresh air.

After washing her face and pulling her hair together into a messy pineapple ponytail, she threw on a white scoop neck tunic tank top, some dark blue shorts and her running shoes. Downstairs, she had a glass of water and then grabbed her sketch pad and drawing pencil from her straw tote bag. Peeking out the window, Nikki saw nothing that alarmed her. She had decided earlier that Perry Evigan had not followed them to the cabin after all. It was just her panicking, unreasonably so. As such, it was likely safe for her to step onto the wraparound deck, where she would do the sketching, before having breakfast with Gavin.

No sooner had she gone out on the deck and began to sketch, observing some ducks and rabbits out and about by the lake, than Nikki heard a sound that she couldn't quite decipher. Realizing it was the cedar deck boards creaking, she turned in that direction only to come face-to-face with her worst nightmare.

Perry Evigan stood there with an eerie grin playing on his lips and sporting a patchy beard, as he said coldly, "Nice to see you again, Nikki. We have some unfinished business to take care of..."

"No, we don't!" she shot back with defiance, glaring at the man who was unmistakable, in spite of being ten years older.

Just as she attempted to use a self-defense technique, then make a run for it and scream at the same time, Nikki was grabbed roughly and felt a needle pierce her neck. Before everything went black, she heard the Gulfport Nightmare Killer remark smugly, "Don't fight it, Nikki. The ketamine I injected you with will make you mine as we get out of here and go to a safe place where we can get down to business uninterrupted."

GAVIN AWOKE WITH a start when he thought he heard the sound of screeching tires. Expecting to find Nikki beside him—in a dreamy sleep after making love much of the night—he instead realized her spot on the bed was empty. For whatever reason, his gut instincts kicked in that something wasn't right. He shot out of bed, slid into some slacks and went in his bare feet looking for her. But he couldn't find her in the cabin.

Where was she? Why didn't she wake him up? How could he have not heard the creaking of the stairs?

Gavin resisted the urge to panic, hoping that Nikki had simply gone outside while not going too far. Hadn't she talked about wanting to sketch the scenery? Maybe she had fallen and hit her head? He opened the door and walked out onto the wraparound porch. At first, he saw nothing that got his attention to suggest Nikki was in trouble. But then, near the side of the deck, he spotted what looked to be…her sketch pad and drawing pencil lying there.

Would she have left them there voluntarily?

Gavin called out to her, "Nikki!" He went around the entire deck on the chance that she was there somewhere and hadn't heard him. But she was nowhere to be found. He called her name again. No answer. Would she really leave him hanging if she were able to speak?

Now it was time for panic to set in.

He stepped off the deck and checked the perimeter of the cabin, but saw no sign of Nikki. Realizing that without his firearm and shoes on, he was at a disadvantage, should she be in danger.

Sprinting back into the cabin, his heart racing, Gavin hurriedly scaled the stairs, finished dressing and grabbed his loaded FN 509 MRD-LE 9mm semiautomatic duty pistol. He went back outside and started to look for Nikki, calling her name, while holding out hope that she wasn't in jeopardy.

But when he reached the dirt road and saw fresh tire tracks, Gavin recalled thinking he'd heard tires screeching when he awoke. It hadn't been his imagination after all. Someone had taken Nikki.

No, not someone.

Perry Evigan had her.

The mere thought that the bastard had kidnapped Nikki

made the hairs curl on the back of Gavin's neck. He needed to regroup and find the woman he'd fallen in love with. Before Evigan was able to murder someone else Gavin cared for.

AT FIRST, Nikki thought she was in some weird dream where everything was fuzzy and nothing was as it seemed. She was trapped under water and sinking fast. As she tried to scream, her mouth filled with muddy water and death seemed imminent. Then she opened her eyes and saw nothing but darkness and felt herself lying in a fetal position in a tight space. She realized she wasn't dreaming at all. She was caught in a living nightmare.

Though groggy, she came to the conclusion that she was trapped inside something… A trunk. And the car was moving.

Everything began to come back to her. She was on the wraparound deck of the log cabin of Gavin's friend—about to sketch the surroundings—when she was accosted by Perry Evigan, who injected her with a date-rape drug.

It was the last thing she remembered. Till now.

He'd kidnapped her and was taking her somewhere. Nikki quickly realized that the trunk emergency release lever had been ripped out. She tried to push and kick open the trunk lid, to no avail. And though she wanted to scream, nothing seemed to come out of her sour throat and dry mouth but a whimper.

Where were they going? Was Gavin aware that she was missing? Or was he still asleep, oblivious to what had happened to her?

Am I going to be able to get out of this alive? Nikki asked herself fearfully. Or would Evigan make good on his pledge of revenge, doing to her whatever ghastly things he had in mind? Finishing with strangling her to death and maybe burying her where she could never be found. And leaving Gavin and her parents to mourn her death, just as they had Brigette's. While their killer remained free to go after other young women, with no end in sight.

This frightening scenario chilled Nikki to the core and was one that she needed to do everything in her power to avoid. Now if only she could overcome the dizziness and trouble breathing in the enclosed space to formulate a plan of action.

PERRY EVIGAN COULD barely believe his good fortune. First, he executed a timely escape from the Mississippi State Penitentiary—dodging every close call in the effort to recapture him. Then, he managed to avoid the fate of fellow escapees, Craig Schneider and Aaron Machado, who literally went up in flames rather than go back inside.

And now, Perry had gotten hold of his prized possession, Nikki Sullivan. He'd found his way to her in Owl's Bay, where she had thought she was safe from him. She had become his for the taking—and he fully intended to do just that—before ending her life once and for all, as he had intended to do a decade ago. He could hear her squirming inside the trunk, hoping to find some miraculous way of breaking free. He was confident that wasn't going to happen.

Perry glanced at the rearview mirror to make sure he wasn't being followed. There was no one behind them. Good. He had dumped the Toyota Corolla Cross he had stolen for a green Dodge Charger GT. By the time they figured out it had been carjacked by him, he would have done what he set out to do with Nikki Sullivan and moved on.

So much for her protector Special Agent Gavin Lynley keeping her safe from harm. Perry laughed at the thought. He remembered learning that Lynley had been dating Brigette Fontana ten years ago—only to come up short in preventing her death. Now he was about to go 0 for 2 in the saving a damsel in distress department.

You lose again, Perry mused wryly, as they neared the destination for his latest kill. He salivated at the thought, knowing it would be even more of a thrill when the deed was done.

"Nikki's missing," Gavin spoke glumly over the speakerphone to Marvin Whitfield while driving.

"What do you mean she's missing?" the director asked, ill at ease.

"He took her," Gavin hated to say, feeling nauseated picturing Nikki in the clutches of the serial killer. "Somehow, Perry Evigan managed to lure Nikki out of the cabin. Or she went out unsuspectingly and he was waiting for her…and kidnapped her."

Whitfield spat out an expletive. "I thought we had him boxed in," he groaned, "if not in custody."

"Instead, Evigan's outfoxed us in being able to slip out of Owl's Bay and track down Nikki." Gavin frowned and sucked in a deep breath, blaming himself for placing her in harm's way and allowing the escaped con to nab Nikki under his watch. "I don't know where he's taken her, but they couldn't have gotten very far," Gavin said, driving in the direction the tire tracks suggested Evigan went.

"Only a few minutes passed before I realized that Nikki was gone."

"Tell me exactly where you are and we'll have the Fugitive Apprehension Strike Team and other law enforcement converge on the area and try to cut Evigan off."

Gavin gave his GPS coordinates and said, "If Evigan is still driving the Toyota Corolla Cross, we should be able to narrow down—"

Whitfield cut him off by saying forlornly, "We found the Toyota a few hours ago. It had been abandoned by Evigan. He's obviously using another vehicle right now."

"Figures," Gavin muttered sarcastically, then remembered Nikki believing she had seen him yesterday at the grocery store, as he approached it. "Let me get back to you. I may be able to pin down what Evigan is driving… and has Nikki inside against her will."

The director sought no explanation as he deferred to Gavin's potential new lead, while both moved into high gear, trying to find Nikki alive, before it was too late.

PACING IN HIS OFFICE, Marvin Whitfield was on pins and needles as he contemplated the dire situation with Perry Evigan. In no way should it have gotten to this point, where this serial killer seemed to be calling the shots. And not him as the Director of Investigations at MDOC. He couldn't let this stand, as the buck stopped with him. Last thing he needed was to have Evigan do to Nikki Sullivan what he did to her friend, Brigette Fontana. Not to mention give Gavin Lynley another reason to shoulder the blame, should this go south on him.

Whitfield wondered if it was wise to send Gavin to do bodyguard duty of the artist. Maybe this was a little too close to home for him, causing the special agent to lower his guard just enough to allow Nikki to slip through his fingers for Evigan to nab. And now had them all at a disadvantage in a race against time to stop him from killing her.

But as the director reconsidered this, he knew deep down that Gavin Lynley was where he needed to be. He had every right to confront the enemy—no matter the cost. And to play a role in rescuing Nikki Sullivan from the grasp of Evigan and his evil intentions.

Whitfield was determined to do everything in his power to stop the escaped convict from continuing to circumvent the law by remaining free to wreak havoc in their state and flaunting this in their faces. He got on his cell phone to speak with the Fugitive Apprehension Strike Team Commander, Eddie Prescott, to talk strategy in converging on Osweka County and holding Perry Evigan accountable for his crimes and bringing him to justice.

Chapter Sixteen

Nikki felt the car driving onto gravel, before coming to a stop. She heard Evigan get out and approach the trunk. Holding her breath, she waited for it to open and have to face her tormentor again.

When the trunk lid was lifted, Perry Evigan stood there smugly, wearing a dark blue fleece pullover hoodie and jeans. His short brown-gray hair was uncombed and his face had become weathered after a decade.

"I see you're awake," he said with a laugh, while holding a gun. She wondered if it was the one he'd used to shoot to death Kenan Fernández. "Good to see I didn't overdo it with the ketamine." She sneered but said nothing as he grabbed her with one hand and pulled her out of the trunk. "Welcome home, Nikki."

It took her a moment to recognize the setting. It was the same two-story Greek Revival house on Robinson Road that he had first brought her and Brigette to ten years ago, after also being drugged. Only now it was overgrown with weeds and looked more dilapidated. Was anyone actually living there these days?

"I see it's all coming back to you now," Perry expressed, grinning wickedly as he clicked together his scuffed brown Chelsea boots. He kept the gun on her and pushed her toward the house. "Get inside and I'll try to make this as painless as possible."

Yeah, right, Nikki told herself doubtingly. She expected it to be just the opposite, knowing that, based on his history—including the rape and murder of Miriam Broderick—the serial killer got his kicks out of inflicting pain and humiliation on his victims, before he strangled them to death with ligatures. Or even his bare hands.

I have to play along for now, Nikki thought, biding her time till she struck back. Or died trying. Assuming Gavin was unable to come to her rescue in the nick of time.

"You won't get away with this, Perry," she spat, if only to try to reach his sense of self-preservation.

He chuckled, shoving her again. "Watch me."

As they neared the porch, Nikki took a quick glance at the shed and then nearby woods, and tried to map out an escape route, should the opportunity present itself.

That thought had to be put on hold as Perry Evigan forced the front door open and made her go inside.

GAVIN FLASHED HIS identification as he said to the grocery store manager in an official tone of voice, "Special Agent Lynley."

Sarah Yarborough, fortysomething and petite, with red hair in an angled short cut and blue eyes behind oval glasses, asked, "How can I help you, Agent Lynley?"

"I need to take a look at your security footage from yesterday, inside and out." He gave her a time frame to work with. "We have reason to believe that an escaped prisoner may have been seen in the area…"

"Sounds scary."

"And for good reason—if it's him," Gavin told her

point-blank, while trying to hold it together, knowing that every second counted where it concerned Nikki's survival.

Sarah furrowed her brow uneasily and said, "Follow me."

She led him through the store to a back room with surveillance equipment. Standing before a laptop, the store manager pulled up security video footage at the store's entrance.

Gavin waited till he saw what—or whom—he was looking for and asked her to stop. "Can you zoom in on that man?"

"Sure." Sarah did just that, giving Gavin a closer look. "Do you recognize him?" she asked.

"Yeah, I'm afraid I do," Gavin muttered, his nose wrinkling in disgust. The man was clearly on edge, his big hazel eyes shifting this way and that, for fear of being recognized, even with the hood of his dark-colored sweatshirt over his head. It was him, undeniably. "His name's Perry Evigan."

Though years removed from when Gavin confronted the serial killer in court, he would recognize Brigette's killer anywhere. Nikki had been right in believing she spotted Evigan at the store yesterday.

I should have trusted her judgment and been better prepared to deal with it when he came for her, Gavin told himself, knowing that if Evigan laid one hand on Nikki, he would never forgive himself.

"I heard about him," Sarah confessed. "Can't believe he was actually here."

"Believe it." Gavin jutted his chin. "Let's switch to the outside surveillance camera..."

"All right."

She pulled up the footage from just after the time Evigan was inside the store and Gavin spotted him walking to a green Dodge Charger GT. He got inside and started to drive away.

"Stop it there!" Gavin ordered her, and asked her to zoom in on the license plate. He took a photo of it on his cell phone and said, "I've seen enough." He knew that with Evigan having a head start on him with his deadly plans for Nikki, there was no time to waste in going after the serial killer before the damage done was irreversible.

MINUTES LATER, Gavin was in his car as he passed along to Jean the license plate number of the green Dodge Charger GT that Perry Evigan had sped off in from the supermarket parking lot the day before.

"Got it," she said and was able to quickly run the plates and determine that the vehicle had been carjacked. "The thirtysomething owner of the Dodge Charger, Karl Shimomura, who was also robbed but not physically harmed, had reported the car stolen at gunpoint by a man wearing a hoodie."

"Perry Evigan," Gavin thought out loud, recalling the hoodie Evigan was wearing at the store, coupled with him being the one who fled in the stolen vehicle.

"We'll issue a BOLO immediately on the Dodge Charger GT," Jean stated, "which shouldn't be too difficult to track down—if Evigan is still in the area—with the tremendous amount of manpower that's out in full pursuit of the escapee."

Gavin twisted his lips. "I've heard it all before," he voiced cynically. "Evigan knows we're onto him—making him all the more dangerous and desperate, as his kidnapping of Nikki was conniving and deliberate."

"If he had wanted to kill her right away, Evigan would have done so," the special agent surmised cautiously. "That tells me Nikki Sullivan is probably still alive."

But not for much longer, unless I can find her in time, Gavin told himself, trying hard not to panic at the thought of being too late. He only needed something to go on for a sense of direction in discovering where Evigan was headed with his captive.

"If the BOLO alert comes up with anything," Gavin told Jean as he drove, "hopefully, I'll be close enough to get to Nikki." Before Evigan could put into action the horrible ordeal he'd put Brigette through, culminating in her death.

THE PLACE HAD a musty smell that suggested it hadn't been lived in for a while, along with the dusty contemporary furnishings and even a few cobwebs that Nikki spotted in corners and hanging from the ceiling. As she was pushed forward across the dark hardwood flooring on the main level, she knew she had to buy time before the escaped serial killer went on the attack.

Rounding on her kidnapper, who was still brandishing the firearm and sizing her up like a piece of meat, Nikki asked point-blank, "It was you who killed Kenan Fernández, wasn't it?"

Evigan cracked a grin. "Yeah, I confess—little good it's going to do you."

"But why?" Not that she needed to know what went on inside the head of an obvious psychopath. However, she was still curious as to what had prompted him to go after Kenan.

"Why? Because I could tell that he wanted you too," Evigan argued. "I saw him through the window at the art gallery. The way he was all up in your face and the way you reacted, told me that the man was a problem. You were mine and I had to eliminate the competition."

Nikki sneered. "Kenan wasn't competition. I rejected his advances and wanted nothing to do with him."

Evigan laughed. "I don't think he saw things that way. Kenan Fernández got what he deserved." Evigan's brow wrinkled. "So too would've Brigette's former boyfriend, Special Agent Lynley, who really rubbed me the wrong way at my trial—just as you did—except for the fact that I wasn't able to get the jump on him without putting my own life at risk. Lucky dude."

Nikki was given a start at the thought that Evigan had wanted Gavin dead apparently as much as he wanted to kill her, in spite of the fact that Gavin had every right to be angered at the sexual assault and murder of his then-girlfriend by Evigan. Nikki could only feel relief that the escaped inmate hadn't succeeded in killing Gavin and destroying his life in the process. Even if she was unable to avoid this fate, with Evigan clearly planning to finish what he started ten years ago.

"Why did you go after Miriam Broderick?" Nikki shot him a hard look. "Was it because of me?" She needed to know if his obsession with her caused Miriam to lose her life, no matter how the forces of fate might work in death.

Evigan threw his head back and roared with laughter. "Sorry to have to tell you this, but the world doesn't just revolve around you, Nikki. The truth is I had sized her up for the kill when I spotted her walking on campus. Miriam fit the bill as someone who met my criteria as a fresh victim—young, attractive, naive and unsuspecting, till it was too late to change what I had in store for her. Much like the predicament you're in now, Nikki—again." He chortled, giving her a lascivious look, ogling her from head to toe, then turning demonic in his facial expression.

I'll see you again someday, Nikki, and finish what I started. Trust me.

She recoiled at the threatening words he'd said to her during his trial and his intentions of making good on his vow, even as she took solace in learning that Miriam's death hadn't been preventable, per se, as Nikki related this to herself and the prison escapee.

I can't give up fighting for my life, Nikki thought resolutely, while eyeing the demented killer and trying to find the slightest chink in his armor.

As though he was reading her mind, Evigan knitted his thick brows and said meanly, "In there."

Nikki looked toward a downstairs bedroom and back at him, her heart pounding. "I know you want to make up for lost time with me, but can't we just talk about this, Perry...?"

"I'm afraid the time for talking is over, Nikki." He made a menacing sound. "Time to get this over with. Now move."

She weighed whether or not to comply. He was still holding the gun on her and seemingly daring her to try to take it from him. Having the serial killer shoot her on the spot and still likely carry out his other sick plans, Nikki thought better of it.

She would obey him while knowing the will to survive was just as strong as ever. Meaning that she would need the courage to do whatever it took for that to happen. Assuming that Gavin would not be able to swoop in and save her—even if Nikki sensed that he was moving heaven and earth to try to do just that.

WITHOUT PREAMBLE, the director said with an edge to his voice, "Fifteen minutes ago, a traffic camera picked up the Dodge Charger GT stolen by Evigan, headed toward Gulfport."

"Gulfport?" Gavin repeated into the cell phone, pensive. It was where Perry Evigan had abducted and taken Nikki and Brigette a decade ago. Why go back to the scene of the crime?

"Yeah," Whitfield confirmed. "With the walls closing in on him, I'm guessing that Evigan may be headed to familiar territory to hide out."

"Not just familiar to him," Gavin remarked, as a light bulb suddenly went off in his head. "Evigan's taking Nikki back to the house where he did his dirty work—and where she was rescued by FBI and other law enforcement."

"Hmm… I'd heard that the house had gone into foreclosure a few years back," the director pointed out. "Don't know what's happened to it since."

"Whoever owns the property or doesn't—my gut instincts tell me that's where we'll find Nikki—and the serial killer," Gavin said worriedly.

Whitfield responded sharply, "I'll notify the Fugitive Apprehension Strike Team, Gulfport Police Department and the rest, along with the Mississippi Department of Public Safety crisis negotiator, to head there."

Knowing he couldn't afford to put Nikki's life solely in their hands, Gavin told him with a sense of sheer determination, "I'm only a few minutes away from Gulfport. I'll meet them there."

"All right. Just be careful, Lynley," he warned. "I don't think I need to remind you that Evigan can be considered armed and dangerous—meaning it puts Nikki Sullivan at that much greater risk as both a victim and human shield."

"I know," Gavin allowed, as he pressed down on the accelerator. "Which is precisely why I need to do this. I won't let Evigan have his way with another woman I want in my life when this is over."

He disconnected and put on even more speed in what had literally become the race of Gavin's career and life, knowing that the life of the woman he loved now hung unsteadily in the balance.

Chapter Seventeen

Nikki was shoved into the room. It was barren, aside from a platform bed with only a soiled mattress, as if left for this moment in time. Dusty faux wood blinds were drawn on the windows. She obviously didn't like where this was going, but had no way out, as he had her at a decided disadvantage.

I need to get him talking more, Nikki told herself, believing that this might be her last chance to not only buy time—that she hoped to sell to Gavin and the others in law enforcement, who were undoubtedly doing everything in their power to locate her and Evigan—but get him to lower his guard somewhat, taking away his inflated sense of invincibility and superiority.

"Take your clothes off, Nikki," Evigan ordered her snappily.

"Okay, okay," she said, turning toward him and seeing that he was still pointing the gun at her. While delaying this demand as long as possible, Nikki stared at her kidnapper and asked curiously, "Just let me ask you a question, Perry… How is it that you didn't end up with the other escaped prisoners at the farmhouse that caught on fire?"

Evigan regarded her thoughtfully and laughed. "I'm a hell of a lot smarter than they were," he said unashamedly.

"They didn't want to separate—strength in numbers and all that silliness. Whereas, that's all I wanted, to go it alone and stick to the game plan I had all along, which was to come after you and take what I was deprived of ten years ago when the cops showed up at my door."

I'll see you again someday, Nikki, and finish what I started. Trust me.

His chilling words once again resonated in her head. Nikki's knees nearly buckled under the weight of his lascivious gawk. Instead, she stood her ground and, peering at Brigette's killer, asked flippantly, "So, now that your wish is about to come true, what happens after that, Perry? Do you intend to go on, sexually assaulting and strangling other women? Or will you simply sail off into the sunset and rest on your laurels? Better yet, maybe you'll turn yourself in, knowing that the authorities will never stop looking for you—wherever you go or try to hide."

Evigan chuckled. "Hadn't really thought that far ahead, to be honest. But if you must know, as a natural-born serial killer, chances are that I'll keep at it for as long as I can—handpicking new victims to go after, feeding my thirst for what I can get from them." His eyes narrowed. "Enough of the questions and answers. Now, take your clothes off! Or I'll rip them off myself."

Nikki pretended that she would voluntarily remove her tank top before stopping. "Maybe you should do it," she dared him. "Or are you afraid to drop the gun and handle me with your bare hands?" She knew this was taking a big risk by incurring his wrath even further and challenging him to get rough with her. But it was better than trying to fight someone who could shoot her at any time.

Evigan took the bait and tucked the gun inside his

waistband. "Okay, if that's what you want, you've got it." He pushed her down hard on the filthy mattress. "This is going to be fun—at least for one of us. I'll even strangle you afterward with my bare hands. Just like I did your friend, Brigette."

He tossed out a sickening laugh as if to really rub it in just how cold-blooded he was as a serial killing monster. The thought of what he did to Brigette and intended to do to her the second time around, only fueled Nikki's anger. Along with her strong will to not give in to victimization again from the same perpetrator. When he relaxed his body while overconfident, and started to bend his knees to lower himself onto the bed, Nikki used the self-defense class mechanism she had been taught. In one quick motion, she lifted her right foot in a running shoe and slammed it as hard as she could against the side of his left knee—immediately dislocating it.

As the leg buckled badly, Evigan screamed an expletive at her and tried to grab his leg to keep from falling. The momentary distraction was enough for Nikki to use her other foot to thrust it with all her might smack-dab against his aquiline nose. The wicked crunching sound told her she had broken it.

While Evigan wailed like a wounded animal as he raised his hands to his bloody face, he lost his balance and fell onto the floor. Not taking any chances of a quick recovery, Nikki wasted no time in jumping off the mattress, knowing she needed to get out of there. She started to race toward the bedroom door, when she felt her leg being grabbed from behind. It was twisted just enough so she lost her balance and tumbled to the floor.

Before she could recover, Nikki was dragged toward

Evigan, who said acrimoniously, "You're going to pay for this, bitch, and I'll enjoy every second of it."

Nikki's pulse raced wildly as she tried to fight off the serial killer, who was now more intent than ever to make her suffer, before strangling her to death.

GAVIN DROVE UP to the Greek Revival-style home on Robinson Road. He spotted the carjacked green Dodge Charger GT parked in the driveway haphazardly. It appeared to be empty. Meaning that most likely Evigan had already forced Nikki inside the house.

I pray I'm not too late, Gavin mused worryingly, as he climbed out of his Chevy Tahoe. Taking the FN 509 MRD-LE 9mm semiautomatic pistol from his tactical thigh leg holster, he checked the Dodge Charger and then approached the foreclosed property cautiously. He refused to believe that Nikki was already dead. There was too much left unsaid for their journey to end prematurely. Evigan could not take away everything that had become most important to Gavin—the chance at love and a lifetime of happiness.

Resting on that optimism and having faith in Nikki's ability to hang in there as long as she possibly could, Gavin stepped onto the porch, which squeaked. In spite of being fearful that he had tipped his hand in warning Evigan that they had company, this didn't prevent him from going full steam ahead as Gavin went inside the broken door that was left partially ajar.

With his pistol out in front of him, he saw signs—such as footprints in the floor dust—that indicated someone was in there. Just as he was about to head up the stairs, Gavin heard Nikki's voice as she called out for help. It was coming from a downstairs bedroom.

He raced toward it and stepped inside, where Gavin saw Perry Evigan halfway atop Nikki on the floor. The serial killer's nose was a bloody mess and one of his legs was awkwardly bent. When Evigan grabbed a handgun from his waist and pointed it at Nikki, Gavin never gave him a chance to use it.

He aimed his pistol and fired twice, hitting Evigan both times in the head, causing brain matter to spray out. The dead man slumped over, falling off Nikki, who was still clothed and appeared unhurt, but clearly shaken as she sat up.

Looking at Gavin, she said softly, "You found me."

"Yeah." He stepped over to her and grinned, helping her to get to her feet, and then hugged her, happy to be able to touch her again. "Are you all right?"

"I think so." Nikki hugged him back for a long moment, then glanced over at Evigan. "Is he…?"

"Yes, Evigan's been neutralized," Gavin spoke confidently. "He won't hurt you or anyone else, ever again."

"That's good to know."

Gavin regarded the serial killer. "Looks like you did quite a number on him before I showed up."

"He really didn't leave me any choice," she said matter-of-factly. "Either fight back or give up. That wasn't an option."

Gavin gave a satisfied smile. "Glad to hear it."

Nikki paused. "He wanted to come after you too."

He arched a brow. "Excuse me?"

"Ever since the trial, Evigan has apparently been caught up in some vindictive vengeance mindset against both of us," she informed him. "But as an armed special agent, you were harder to corner. Though he would likely have never given up trying."

"Wow." Gavin let that roll around in his head for a moment. The idea that Evigan wanted to put him and Nikki in the grave, alongside Brigette, only made it more comforting that he had been stopped cold, before carrying out the rest of his agenda. "The man was obviously the worst kind of human being. Neither of us have to watch our backs anymore, where Evigan's concerned."

Nikki's voice broke as she uttered, "It's a relief, for sure." Her eyes watered. "I thought I might never see you again."

"That wasn't going to happen," Gavin assured her with a straight face. Never mind that, at times, that frightening thought had crossed his mind too. "Not if I had anything to say about it."

"He was waiting for me outside the cabin when I went onto the wraparound deck to sketch the landscape," Nikki explained.

Gavin nodded. "I gathered as much." He only wished he had gone out there with her. And had been able to take out Evigan sooner.

"Before I could react, Evigan had injected me with ketamine and thrown me into the trunk of his car—and brought me here." She looked at Gavin curiously. "How did you figure it out anyway?"

He turned to Evigan and what was left of his head, before Gavin decided that Nikki didn't need to see any more of the man who kidnapped and tried to kill her. "I'll explain in a moment," he told her, taking Nikki's hand to lead her out of the room. Then he said, "You were right about seeing Evigan at the grocery store. After he abducted you, I had a hunch and went back to the store to take a look at their surveillance video. I saw not only Evigan inside, but outside—where he got into a green Dodge Charger GT. Found out that it was carjacked. The vehicle was picked up heading toward Gulfport. I was able to put two and two together that he was taking you here—the scene of the original crimes against you…and Brigette."

"Your instincts were spot-on," Nikki declared. "In his warped mind, Evigan wanted to try and re-create what happened ten years ago—only this time succeeding in his plans to finish me off. Just like he killed Brigette."

"But Evigan failed again," Gavin told her, with a catch to his voice. "He overplayed his hand and lost. Brigette can now have the peace she has long sought. And so can we, Nikki."

She nodded with teary eyes, and said quietly, "It's what I'd always hoped for."

"Same here." Gavin gazed into her eyes soulfully as they heard the sounds of sirens approaching. "But there was always something else I'd always wished for—"

"Oh…" Nikki met his eyes. "What's that?"

"To truly fall in love with someone and be able to tell her that."

"Oh," she repeated. "Is that what you're saying to me?"

"Yes, it is." Gavin's voice fell an octave. "I have fallen in love with you, Nikki Sullivan. Not just young love like I may have felt for Brigette," he made clear, "but adult love for a beautiful and talented artist, who gets me and made me get her. I never thought it would happen this fast, but it has and you need to know that."

"There's something you need to know too," Nikki said, and took his hands, her own trembling. "I think I've been in love with you for the past ten years—or since we were first introduced. But I tried to ignore it for obvious reasons. I felt all along that there was a real connection there, even if your attention was on someone else. After Brigette's death and being blamed for it by you, I thought our moment had passed. That seemed even more the case after the trial, when it seemed like I would never see you again. Then, just days ago—which somehow seems like a year—you showed up at my house…"

"And the rest, as they say, is history," Gavin finished, while looking squarely toward the future, elated to hear that she loved him too and had for some time.

"Yeah." She flashed her teeth. "Something like that."

"And like this," he said, as Gavin cupped her cheeks and they kissed, before putting everything on hold when the Fugitive Apprehension Strike Team and support team showed up and took over the crime scene.

THREE MONTHS LATER, Gavin was driving his Chevrolet Tahoe, with Jean O'Reilly in the passenger seat. They were en route to the Mississippi Department of Corrections Central Office headquarters to discuss with the director of investigations an ongoing probe into gang violence and narcotic violations in the state's prison system.

"Director Whitfield will be happy to know we're making serious progress in getting to the root of the problem and offering constructive solutions," Jean said.

"You think?" Gavin suspected that making progress and really rooting out the dual problems of gangs and drug-related offenses among inmates were two entirely different things that Whitfield, a stickler for actual results, likely wouldn't have much trouble differentiating.

"Hey, have you forgotten how we nailed Titus Malfoy to the wall and made Whitfield look good in the process?"

"I remember." Gavin considered that the probation officer they had investigated for embezzlement and other crimes had pleaded guilty and implicated another probation officer and a parole agent for the bargain. Whitfield had used this to tighten procedures and accountability for those working in these fields in the MDOC.

"Then there's Perry Evigan and the other escapees that came to a satisfactory conclusion under the director's watch," she mentioned.

Gavin thought about Evigan and just how close he came to murdering Nikki—to add to the eleven other women he strangled to death and the four men he killed as well for good measure. The fact that Evigan was now dead and buried gave Gavin only a limited amount of placation. His death could never bring back Brigette or the other victims. But it could bring closure to survivors, such as Nikki, who had gotten an added measure of payback in shattering Evigan's nose and messing up his leg, before the serial killer's time on Earth ran out.

A firearms examiner was able to positively link the SIG Sauer P365 9mm pistol Perry Evigan tried to shoot Nikki with to the murder of Kenan Fernández, to tie up one loose end. Another was to hold those responsible for the prison escape of Evigan, Craig Schneider and Aaron Machado accountable—with Whitfield reassigning Mississippi State Penitentiary superintendent, Crystal Rawlings, and warden, Zachary Livingston, in an effort to reduce the chances of this from happening again in the future. Whitfield went public with this to show both his commitment to prison reform and to take credit for the fugitives being taken off the streets.

"I take your point," Gavin told Jean, with a slight grin. "Maybe we can score some points with the director—and vice versa."

"Yes, I'm game for a basket or two, if you are." She laughed. A minute later Jean asked him, "So, when do you plan to pop the question?"

Gavin glanced her way. "Pop the question?" he asked, as though befuddled.

"Uh, ask Nikki to marry you?"

He didn't need to give this any thought. "As a matter of fact, I plan to do it today."

Jean's eyes widened. "Seriously?"

"Yeah. It's time." Gavin knew, and already felt giddy about tying the knot with the woman he was in love with. "I just hope she says yes."

"There is that." Jean gave a chuckle. "From what I've seen of you two, the *yes* part is a mere formality, Lynley."

He grinned crookedly, while eager to put that to the test.

AT THE OWL'S BAY FITNESS CENTER on Tenth Street, Nikki was on a treadmill, enjoying a good workout. She welcomed being able to do one of the things she loved most in staying fit, without the ominous shadows of Kenan Fernández and, even more, Perry Evigan, hanging over her. She was still coming to terms with the fact that the serial killer who murdered her best friend and was on the verge of sending her to an early grave as well—had Gavin not intervened—was now dead himself. Meaning that he wouldn't get the chance to escape from prison again to wreak havoc on her life or the lives of other innocent people.

Justice was definitely served here, Nikki told herself, as she turned toward her friend, Blair Roxburgh, who had been there for her throughout the ordeal that included them losing another friend to Evigan, Miriam Broderick.

"Having trouble keeping up, are we?" Blair joked, as Nikki had inadvertently slowed down her pace during the reverie.

"Sorry about that." She laughed, while picking it up again. "I'll try not to drift off any more."

"You're entitled," Blair said. "Especially if you're fantasizing about that hot boyfriend of yours, Special Agent Lynley."

Nikki colored. "Maybe I was," she confessed, at least to some degree. "Can you blame me?" She knew that Blair, who had recently gotten engaged to her boyfriend, Oliver Pascal, was hoping Nikki and Gavin would follow suit. Though they were rotating spending long weekends at her place and his, the subject of marriage hadn't come up. For her part, Nikki was more than ready and willing to walk down the aisle with the man she loved. But pressuring Gavin to want the same wasn't in her nature. Should it be?

"Not one bit." Blair grabbed her water bottle and took a sip. "You know, you could just go out on a limb and ask Gavin for his hand in marriage. I'm guessing that he would never want you to get away."

"Hmm..." Nikki drank water thoughtfully. Was Gavin ready for that? Or was he content to keep things as they were for now, while still expressing his love for her? "We'll have to see about that," she told her friend noncommittally. "All I know for certain at the moment is that I never want to let Gavin slip away from me."

"That's never going to happen," Blair reassured her. "Whatever else I may think of your special agent, he definitely knows a great thing when he sees and touches it."

"Ditto." Nikki cherished the thought of a future together with Gavin, in whatever form both could live with.

WHEN GAVIN SHOWED up at Nikki's cottage that evening with a dozen long-stemmed red roses, it was fully intended to woo her. "For you," he said coolly.

She blushed. "Thank you." Her nose took in the fragrance. "They're lovely."

"So are you." Gavin grinned, resisting the urge to kiss her for the time being.

Nikki smiled. "I'll go put these in some water."

"Before you do—" he lifted one rose from the bouquet that held something hidden in a leaf and removed it "—you might want to see if this ring fits…" Falling to one knee, Gavin held up the 2.5 carat princess-cut engagement ring with a diamond band in platinum and said affectionately, "Nikki Sullivan, I don't think it's any secret that I've fallen madly in love with you. That's only grown these past few months. I'd like nothing more than to make it official by becoming your husband and father to any children that come our way. Will you marry me and make my happiness level off the charts?"

Without ado, Nikki cried, "Yes, yes, I'll marry you, Gavin Lynley. I love you too, just as madly!" She put a hand to her mouth at the joy of the moment, then stretched it out for him to slide the ring onto.

"I'm delighted to hear that," he professed, and put the ring on her finger. "How does it feel?"

"Like it belongs," she uttered, gazing at the engagement ring admiringly. "Like we belong."

"We do." Gavin got to his feet, finding it difficult to take the smile off his face. "For the rest of our lives," he swore.

"Yes, the rest of our lives," Nikki repeated blissfully. She tilted her face upward. "Kiss me and we'll make this official."

"With pleasure." He puckered his lips and brought them upon hers that opened slightly in anticipation for that sweet kiss, which was stirring and gave Gavin something to definitely look forward to time and time again. He broke their lip-lock just long enough to say sweetly, "I think that definitely makes our engagement to marry and live happily thereafter official."

Epilogue

Gavin watched as his sister, Lauren, and her husband, Rory Nolden, along with their two little girls, Ellen and Miley, appeared on the laptop screen for a Zoom video chat.

"Hey, everyone," Gavin said evenly.

Ellen and Miley, seven and eight, respectively, both with long curly dark hair and brown eyes, and resembling both parents, said in unison, "Hi, Uncle Gavin."

"What's up, man," Rory said merrily, wearing round reading glasses over brown eyes. His brown hair was styled in a spiky quiff cut.

Lauren, who had already picked up on his closeness to Nikki during other conversations, still looked on with anticipation, behind her own geometric-shaped glasses, when she said wryly, "It's so nice to visit with my big brother. Anything special happening in your life these days?"

Gavin laughed. "As a matter of fact, there is…" He took a breath while standing over the marble countertop in Nikki's kitchen. "I wanted you all to be the first to know that I've asked Nikki to marry me…"

"Did she say yes?" Miley asked animatedly.

"Yeah, did she?" Ellen pressed impatiently.

"Come on, out with it," Lauren demanded.

Gavin chuckled. "I thought I should let Nikki tell you herself."

Nikki, who had been standing just out of view of the laptop's camera, moved beside him. "Hey, guys!" She flashed a brilliant smile and stated enthusiastically, "I said yes!" She lifted her hand to show off the engagement ring for everyone to see.

"Congratulations," Lauren said lovingly. "I'm so happy for you both and applaud you, Nikki, for finally being able to make an honest man out of my brother."

Nikki chuckled. "Believe me when I tell you, the pleasure is all mine. Well, maybe a little bit is left over for Gavin."

He laughed, kissing her on the cheek and giving them an opportunity to get to know one another better now that they were about to become family.

ON HER WEDDING DAY, Nikki had butterflies in her stomach with the wonderful anticipation she felt in knowing that she would be spending the rest of her life married to Gavin Lynley. She only wished in an odd way that her first best friend, Brigette, were alive to be there. Though Brigette and Gavin were once an item, Nikki was certain that Brigette would have wanted them both to be happy in her absence.

The wedding was held outdoors on a gorgeous and sunny day in Jackson, Mississippi, where Nikki and Gavin would live. They had already begun home shopping, in search of a property that both could put their stamp on as a place to raise a family. Nikki was thrilled that Jackson was also a wonderful place for artists. She'd already begun to establish herself there with a few pieces on display at various art galleries.

Nikki felt honored that her stepfather had agreed to give her away and was already bonding with Gavin—as both were into jazz music and such great artists as Billie Holiday, Duke Ellington and Sarah Vaughan. Blair was Nikki's maid of honor and the bridesmaids were Gavin's sister, Lauren, and his equally beautiful cousins, Madison and Annette. With Lauren's daughters, Miley and Ellen, serving as the flower girls. All had been very welcoming in having Nikki join their family.

Gavin had asked his college friend and log cabin owner, Jake Kendrick, to be his best man, while choosing his handsome cousins in law enforcement, like Gavin—Scott, Russell and Caleb Lynley—to be his groomsmen. Nikki was elated to be on the threshold of becoming a Lynley herself and hoped to have at least one son to carry on the family name for the next generation, joining their cousins.

As her stepfather walked her down the aisle, Nikki felt beautiful in a white floral lace, V-neck sleeveless mermaid gown with a side cut and white peep-toe high heel sandals. When she stood before her fiancé, Nikki was enamored with him, as he was resplendent in a black tuxedo and matching patent leather Oxfords.

"You look incredible," Gavin told her, a generous grin on his handsome face.

Her teeth shone. "So do you."

"You ready for this?"

"I've never been more ready," Nikki told him, meaning it with all her heart.

"Same here," Gavin promised her.

They brought their own vows to read and did so without missing a beat, while gazing into each other's eyes. When they were finished and exchanged diamond wedding bands, the female pastor pronounced them husband and wife and gave them permission to kiss one another. It was short, sweet and satisfying to Nikki as her husband took her by the hand and they headed down the aisle joyously. Nikki stopped briefly to give her mother a hug.

"I'm so proud of you, Nikki," she told her tearfully. "And Gavin too."

"Thanks, Mom." Nikki received a kiss on the cheek from her parents and then proceeded on with the man she intended to have a great life with as Mrs. Gavin Lynley.

Their wedding night was everything Nikki could have asked for and so much more. It felt like both the first time and a comfortable sense of familiarity that she looked forward to relishing for years to come.

FOR THEIR TWO-WEEK HONEYMOON, Gavin surprised Nikki by fulfilling her dream of going on a cruise. He wanted to make the start of their marriage a memorable occasion and a shared adventure that could propel them to further outings in keeping the romance alive through the years.

As the riverboat cruised the Upper and Lower Mississippi River, its ports of call included fascinating small towns in multiple states including Missouri, Tennessee, Minnesota, Louisiana and, of course, Mississippi. In each place, they enjoyed the cuisine, culture and music of the locals, all while discovering more about each other.

Halfway through the voyage, Gavin and Nikki stood on the private veranda in their stateroom, while appreciating picturesque landscapes and astounding views of the Mississippi. They were sipping Manhattan cocktails, when Gavin had to ask, "So, is this everything you thought a riverboat cruise would be?"

"How could it not be?" Nikki beamed. "Getting married and then taking this journey with the man of my dreams is more than I could ever have asked for."

"Really?" Gavin was delighted to hear her say that, eager to please in every way he could.

"Well, actually, there is one other thing I could think of that just might truly make it complete."

He tasted the cocktail and gazed curiously into her lovely eyes. "And what might that be?" he asked nervously.

"Only this—" Nikki stood on her tiptoes and laid a mouthwatering kiss on his lips that left Gavin breathless and wanting for more.

"Oh, was that all?" he quipped once their mouths had separated.

"Hmm…" She licked her lips. "Well, maybe there is one last bit of business to absolutely make the cruise unforgettable…"

Gavin regarded her keenly. "Name it."

"In that case," Nikki said flirtatiously, "here's precisely what I had in mind…"

She whispered sweet and sensual words in his ear and the rest spoke for itself.

* * * * *

Look for the previous books in R. Barri Flowers's miniseries, The Lynleys of Law Enforcement, available now wherever Harlequin Intrigue books are sold!

Special Agent Witness
Christmas Lights Killer
Murder in the Blue Ridge Mountains
Cold Murder in Kolton Lake
Campus Killer

SPECIAL EXCERPT FROM

HARLEQUIN
INTRIGUE

An overworked district attorney's Christmas getaway takes a deadly turn when she discovers the body of a woman who looks just like her. Can the local sheriff uncover the truth and keep her safe before she becomes a ruthless killer's next victim?

Read on for a sneak preview of
Christmas Peril on the Oregon Coast,
an online read in R. Barri Flowers's miniseries
The Lynleys of Law Enforcement.

Chapter One

To Hannah Brewster, winning wasn't necessarily everything. Well, truthfully, it was a pretty big deal. Especially when winning another high-profile murder trial as an assistant district attorney in Josephine County, Oregon. Six months ago, she'd sent a man to prison for a road rage incident that left two people dead. Three months back, she'd put a woman away for murdering her lover in cold blood. Then a week ago, Hannah got a conviction of a notorious serial killer who had terrorized young women for years in Southern Oregon. Now he'd spend the rest of his life behind bars.

Feeling the weight of her successes in court, in spite of the triumphs and having recently ended a relationship that was going nowhere, Hannah needed a break. So, on the spur of the moment, she packed a few things and rented a waterfront cabin in Pineberry Bay on the Oregon coast. There, she intended to spend the Christmas holiday for some real rest, relaxation, reading and, her favorite pastime for staying in shape, hiking. As for the latter, she wanted to take full advantage of the Oregon Coast Trail accessible in the town, with its eye-catching forested pathways and amazing headlands.

Driving a blue Subaru Ascent down US-199 South for

the two-hour drive, Hannah arrived at her destination. She immediately fell in love with the cozy one-bedroom cabin overlooking the Rogue River with a wraparound deck, plenty of floor-to-ceiling windows, a fully stocked kitchen and pretty much all the comforts of her luxury condominium. There was even a decorated miniature pine Christmas tree and other decorations throughout the cabin to bring in the holiday spirit.

After unpacking and calling her sister, Karen, to let her know she had made it safely, Hannah dressed appropriately for a short hike and tied her long, curly raven hair into a high ponytail before heading out. She imagined that she would serendipitously meet a handsome and fit fellow vacationer who was gainfully employed, just as available as her and could magically sweep her off her feet for a lifetime of wedded bliss together.

Dream on, Hannah thought as she quickly came back down to earth, making her way across the well-worn path through old-growth forests of tall cedar and spruce trees. She refused to set her sights too high, having been there, done that, with less than satisfying results. She only wanted to enjoy nature and reflect on where she saw her career headed, with more cases on the docket to try shortly after the new year began.

When she heard what sounded like the crunching of leaves in the near distance, Hannah wondered if there were other hikers she would run into. She turned her blue eyes in the direction of the sounds, which seemed to be moving away from her steadily. Hannah gave a sigh of relief—she was fearful of being attacked. She was glad now that she had taken self-defense classes. Perhaps the culprit was only one of the many harmless wildlife species occupying the region, she considered, as there was no sign of a human running away.

Just as she let her guard down again, Hannah was stopped cold in her tracks. Lying off the trail in a pool of blood was a dark-haired female. The woman's big blue eyes were wide-open but blank. Apart from the likelihood that she was dead, it occurred to Hannah uneasily that the woman looked an awful lot like her.

Chapter Two

Cranmoore County Sheriff Caleb Lynley had to admit that the deceased woman—tentatively identified through the driver's license she was carrying as Aimee Winterburn, age thirty-two—did bear a strong resemblance to Hannah Brewster, the person who discovered the victim.

But the ADA, alive and well, had a more heart-shaped face with blue eyes that Caleb found to be arresting. He imagined what her dark hair would look like when not in a ponytail.

He probably shouldn't be regarding her in romantic terms but couldn't help himself as a normal and healthy thirty-four-year-old male, who had gone too long without adult companionship. He only wished that Hannah Brewster's holiday in Pineberry Bay hadn't taken such a wrong turn right off the bat. Hopefully, the rest of her vacation would not be quite as dramatic.

"I can see a slight resemblance," he told her, seeking to downplay any possible conclusions that might be drawn from what appeared to be a homicide, based on the apparent head injury and positioning of the body.

Hannah wrinkled her dainty nose. "Not sure what to make of that, honestly—slight resemblance or more—other than mere coincidence. What else could it be?"

"Exactly." Caleb's gray eyes studied her beneath his campaign hat. "Do you have any reason to believe otherwise?" He hadn't actually been familiar with her as a prosecutor to know if she had any enemies who might come after her.

"Not really."

She seemed to hedge, prompting him to ask curiously, "Who knew you were going to spend your Christmas vacation in Pineberry Bay?"

Hannah considered this and replied, "Just my sister, Karen, and her husband, Steve, along with my boss, Josephine County District Attorney Adam Victorino." Hannah made a face. "I'm pretty sure that none of them shared this information."

"Okay. So we'll assume that this wasn't a case of mistaken identity." Caleb glanced at the crime scene, which was being processed by a CSI Unit, while they awaited the arrival of the medical examiner to remove the body. Gazing back at the ADA, he asked, "Did you see anyone else or hear anything before you discovered the victim?"

"I heard someone—or something—in the distance, but didn't see anything. Whoever did this must have heard me coming and ran off and out of sight."

"And a good thing at that," Caleb had to say. "Otherwise, the unsub may have come after you, too." Even if she was not the intended victim.

"True." Hannah's shoulders slumped thoughtfully. "If you're through with me, Sheriff Lynley—"

He nodded, giving her permission to leave. "Where can I reach you, Ms. Brewster?" he asked, in case an official follow up statement was needed.

"I rented a log cabin by the river on Wattson Lane."

"My daughter and I live on that street," Caleb told her, aware that there were a few rental properties as his neighbors, whether he liked it or not.

"Must be nice." Hannah smiled briefly as she assessed him. She gave him her cell phone number and said, "Hope it doesn't take too long to solve this case."

"Assuming you hiked from the cabin, I'll have one of my deputies walk you back, to be on the safe side."

She nodded. He didn't necessarily want to alarm her by suggesting she might be in danger, but couldn't dismiss the possibility that the ADA may have been a target.

Caleb watched her walk off and then turned his attention back to the crime scene, while having an uneasy feeling that there was more to it than met the eye.

Chapter Three

Hannah had to admit that the sheriff was not at all hard on the eyes. Just the opposite, in fact. Even in his full uniform, she could see that Caleb Lynley was a tall physical specimen. Beneath the campaign hat, which he'd removed briefly, thick dark hair was in curls and stylishly short on the sides and she loved the depth of his gray eyes and his square-jawed face.

The man was definitely her type, were the stars to line up in an ideal world. It wasn't lost on Hannah that Caleb spoke of having a daughter, whom he lived with. But there was no mention of a wife or girlfriend. Perhaps she had somehow slipped his mind?

No matter. Romancing the sheriff was certainly not foremost on her mind as Hannah returned to the cabin, having been a witness after the fact to what appeared to be a homicide. She thanked the deputy, a fiftysomething, crimson-haired woman who spent their time together on the trail talking about her husband, kids and grandkids. This reminded Hannah that she had yet to experience any of these things, through no fault of her own.

She undid her hair, poured herself a glass of red wine

and sat on a rustic log sofa, where Hannah called her sister for a video chat.

Karen Nelson was two years older and looked like Hannah, aside from having mid-length blond hair in a layered cut. “Hey,” she said cautiously.

“Hey.” Hannah adjusted her position on the sofa. “Something bad happened.”

“What?”

She told Karen about finding the dead woman whom the sheriff believed had been murdered, causing her sister to remark with horror, “That’s awful!”

Hannah didn’t disagree and had to say, “But here’s the really weird part… The victim reminds me of myself, physically speaking. It was almost as if I was the one who was supposed to be killed, strange as that sounds.”

“It does sound strange, Hannah. Don’t even go there,” her sister begged. “I know you may have rubbed some people the wrong way in the courtroom, but tracking you to a coastal getaway to murder you is a real stretch. Besides, no one knew you were going there, other than family and the district attorney.”

“You’re right on both counts,” Hannah concurred and sipped the wine musingly. “I know I’m probably just letting my imagination run away with itself.”

“I think so.”

“I’ll feel better when Sheriff Caleb Lynley solves the case.”

“I’m sure he will,” Karen told her. “In the meantime, try not to let this ruin your trip. After working so hard for the DA’s office, you’ve earned a break.”

“I know.” Hannah forced a smile. “I’d better let you go.”

"Be careful."

"I will," Hannah promised, and then disconnected. She sipped the wine and wondered why this still had her on edge.

Don't miss
Christmas Peril on the Oregon Coast
by R. Barri Flowers,
available online now at
www.Harlequin.com